—Lovel

SHY GIRL

MELINDA HOUSTON

PAN MACMILLAN

First published 1991 by Pan Macmillan Publishers Australia

This Lovelines edition published 1993 by
Pan Macmillan Children's Books
A division of Pan Macmillan Publishers Limited
Cavaye Place London SW10 9PG
and Basingstoke
Associated companies throughout the world

ISBN 0 330 33003 9

9 8 7 6 5 4 3 2 1

A CIP catalogue record for this book is available from
the British Library

This is a work of fiction. All characters and events in the story are
imaginary and any resemblance to any person living or dead is
purely coincidental.

Typeset by Trade Graphics
Printed by Cox & Wyman Ltd, Reading

Chapter 1

I felt sick. Really — like I was going to vomit. As the car reached the top of the hill, I could see the sea out of the corner of my eye and I said to Mum:

'Turn left.'

She slowed down and reached out her little finger for the indicator and turned and looked at me politely. She's very polite, my mum.

'Pardon?'

'Turn left here and just keep going. Don't mind the splash.'

She started to raise her eyebrows and crinkle them together (her puzzled look), then saw the sea too and gave my hand a squeeze.

'It's going to be all right, love. You'll see. Lots of people your own age, a proper school. In a week's time you'll be loving it.'

I didn't say anything. I couldn't, my teeth were clenched so tight. It's funny, I'd never thought of school. When Dad had told us about the move, we'd all been really excited. Living in the city! Not a week in a daggy hotel-motel in Port Augusta, but a house of our own in a real city. Shops, public transport, newspapers on the same day they were printed, a letter box, colour television. Civilisation.

School never crossed my mind.

Then suddenly we were in front of it, and I not only felt sick, I felt like I was going to cry. Which would've been a real disaster. So I just sat there with my eyes closed, totally paralysed. I felt kind of dumb, but at the time I really couldn't seem to move.

Then Mum leaned over.

'Come on, Katie — it's really not that bad. You know you can do absolutely anything you put your mind to.' And she squeezed my hand again. The combination of the squeeze and the pep-talk — which I'd been able to recite word for word since I was about twelve — got me going. I took a deep breath and got out of the car.

'Ladies and gentlemen, this is Katherine Anderson — but we're to call you Kate, is that right?' The teacher looked at me with that gooey smile teachers produce when they're trying to be friendly. (City or country or on the moon, teachers just seem to be the same everywhere.)

I nodded. Thirty pairs of eyes were boring into me. I wanted to die.

'Find yourself a seat, Kate. For the first few lessons we're having a bit of a catch-up on what we did last year, and this morning we're talking about the principal of *caveat emptor* — which means ... ?'

The sixty eyes finally took their beam off me — they all looked down at their books instead so they wouldn't have to answer the question. I knew the answer, but wild horses couldn't have dragged it out of me just then. Finally the girl sitting next to me said, 'Buyer beware.'

'Thank you, Nikki. Buyer beware. Jamie, would you like to give us a run-down on the implications of the phrase?'

'Uh — no — not really.'

This got my eyes — and everyone else's — up from our books. There were snickers from round the room, and I saw a tall lanky guy in a baseball cap grinning and shrugging his shoulders in a cute sort of way. Jamie, obviously.

The teacher didn't seem to mind too much, he just said in a flat kind of voice, 'Let me re-phrase that. To the best of your ability, Jamie, explain to us what the term *caveat emptor* means in practice.'

The guy Jamie started bumbling through his explanation, and I snuck a look around the room. The girl next to me, Nikki, was short, with thick dark hair in a ponytail and no make-up. She looked okay, but it was pretty easy to see who was who. Nikki sat in a clump of four other girls, all with clean hair and uniforms and short, clean fingernails and unchewed biros. I christened them the Studiers. There was another group of girls with long perms or short spikes, short skirts and Docs instead of regulation school-shoes. The Good Time Girls. They were whispering to each other and egging on Jamie, who sat with the tanned muscly, athletic types. The Jocks.

And then there was me. The hayseed. My stomach started to churn over again.

At last the class ended, and as I was going out the door the teacher came over to me.

'Do you need any help, Kate?'

'No thanks,' I croaked brightly. Of course I did. I had no bloody idea where to go or what to do next — but it's kind of a hard thing to confess. So the teacher just nodded and laid on the gooey smile again and collected up his things.

'What have you got next?' It was the girl Nikki.

'Uh ... ' I fumbled with my books. There was a timetable in there somewhere. Then I

4

realised I was blocking the doorway, looking and sounding like a complete moron. My face went bright red. It felt so hot it's a wonder my hair didn't self-combust or something. Finally I got myself out of the doorway, got my timetable out from between my books, and managed to say, 'Economics.'

'Me too. I'll show you where to go.'

I'll say this for the Studiers. They have a lot of sympathy for dorks.

After economics, Nikki introduced me to some of her friends, who asked me polite questions about who I was and where I came from and where I was living now. It turned out none of them live nearby — which made me half disappointed and half relieved. They were nice girls — nice enough not to mind me being clumsy and tongue-tied and going bright red every time someone spoke to me — but they were also really, really boring. Which I guess is kind of a sad reflection on my character as much as anything. But there it is.

At lunch time I was shown to my locker. The one on my left belonged to one of the Good Time Girls from my Legal Studies class. I guess I stared at her a bit — I couldn't help it. She stared at me too. I felt like I was in a zoo — only I wasn't sure which side of the bars I was on. So I stared at her for a bit, then (naturally) started to feel my face going pink. I can usually tell the colour of my face from its temperature, like the fire danger warnings on the news. Mum reckons I'll grow out of it, but I don't know if I can stand the wait.

'You're Kate, right?'

'I'm Kate.' At least my voice sounded reasonably normal.

She looked at me for a bit longer, and I could almost hear the cogs turning over. Then she did this kind of half-grin.

'I'm Lucy.'

'Hi.'

'And I'm Jamie.'

For a split second I panicked — surrounded by Cool People! Then I got a grip on myself and just said, 'Hi.'

It was the guy in the baseball cap. He was kind of cute. I liked his face. It was just a nice, regular face, not too handsome, not too ugly.

'Do you know where to get your lunch?'

I shook my head.

'Come on then.'

Lucy came with us. She looked a lot like I'd always wanted to look. Tall, with long legs and long, black, curly hair halfway down her back. Except that I'd always wanted to be black, too. Sort of a cross between Lisa Bonet and

Grace Jones. Instead I was short and white and definitely didn't have long legs, and my hair wasn't really curly or really straight either. Not that I was ugly or anything. I just wasn't a stunner like Lucy.

'What did you think of Mark's party on Saturday?' she was saying.

'It was okay. You looked like you were having a pretty good time.'

She laughed. 'I was pretty drunk. But did you see Geoff?'

'Yeah! What was the matter with him? He looked like someone had hit him over the head with a club!'

'He was so stoned.' She said 'so' like it had about ten o's — 'soooooo'.

Jamie just grunted.

'He reckons his brother got it for him — you know, Martin.'

'Martin Jenkins' going to get himself into trouble one of these days. Or somebody else.'

'Jamie, sometimes you're so — square!'

He turned and raised one eyebrow at her, but Lucy just laughed and pulled his cap down over his eyes.

Meanwhile I was trotting along a respectful couple of paces behind them. If your legs are less than long it's sometimes kind of difficult to

7

keep up. And apart from that, I really didn't want to get into that conversation. Parties? Stoned? I knew about it all, of course — I'd read *Go Ask Alice*. And the American kids at Woomera had parties, but we were never invited. They stuck to themselves pretty much. I wasn't one hundred per cent sure what really went on at them. Then Lucy looked over her shoulder at me.

'We decided to have a whole lot of parties early in the year — figure we won't get the chance later on. So we're kind of taking it in turns till the study catches up with us.'

'Or our parents,' added Jamie.

My heart really sank now. Would they expect me to do something? Or maybe I wouldn't be invited at all. I didn't know which was worse. I didn't know what to say either, so I just smiled and gave this dumb little laugh like I knew what they were talking about.

Lucky looked at me kind of strangely, but Jamie just said, 'Well, here we are.'

I made it through the rest of the day. Just. I soon discovered that by deserting Nikki and her crowd for Lucy and Jamie and those guys at lunch time, Nikki et al had decided I wasn't worth the effort. And by hanging round with Nikki and her crowd in the morning, not to mention generally behaving like a jerk, I'd kind of made Lucy feel the same way. She kept giving me these looks every time I ran into her like I had a big wart on the end of my nose or something. It wasn't that she wasn't friendly. She just kept looking at me like I was a freak. Which didn't make me feel so good. So when at dinner Dad asked me how my 'first day at school' went, I didn't exactly know what to say.

'The work's about the same,' I mumbled round my salad.

'And what are the other kids like?'

'Okay.'

'Made any friends yet?'

About forty-nine degrees, and just about the colour of the inside of a strawberry. My face, that is.

'Any nice boys?'

Sixty-eight degrees, and climbing. My dad's pretty keen for me to have a boyfriend, for some reason. Also, when I'm older, to go to cocktail parties and mix with famous writers and film-makers. Fat chance. Do people even have cocktail parties, outside Bette Davis films? And as I thought about Lucy, (who thought I was a freak), and Nikki (who thought I was a snob), and going back to that great, grey, ugly school day after day after day after day I started to feel completely desperate. How was I going to do it? When I didn't say anything Mum and Dad looked at me, sort of surprised. I just couldn't speak. I couldn't eat. I just wanted to crawl into bed and never ever come out again.

Yeah. Living in the city was going to be just great.

Chapter 2

Absolutely anything

You can do absolutely anything you put your mind to. I'd started chanting it to myself on the way to school. I'm not sure it made things any better but it sort of hypnotised me. I didn't panic quite so much. It was funny. When I really thought about it, nothing so terrible happened at school. It's not like people whispered and pointed and called me names or tried to trip me up in the corridor. The Studiers smiled and nodded to me in the corridor. Sometimes they were extra-friendly and said thing like 'Hello' or 'Hi, Kate'. That was okay. You know, it wasn't like I felt I had to be friends with everybody.

And Lucy — well, how can I describe it? She was kind of funny. Strange, that is. Sometimes she'd act like I was her best friend ever — she'd come up to me before school and tell me some confidential story about people I didn't know, and laugh a lot. And I'd kind of laugh along, even though I had no idea what she was talking about. And then at other times she'd whisper to her other friends and look at me out of the corner of her eye at the same time. I could never work out whether she was talking about me, or she wanted me to think she was talking about me, or just that she wanted me to notice she had really important secrets that were too big to be shared with me. I don't know. Funny girl.

So, I still didn't feel too good about going to school. In fact, every night when I went to bed I'd sort of wish that I'd die in my sleep or something. Maybe wake up with an interesting incurable illness. Anything so I didn't have to get up and put on that dumb uniform and go and pretend everything was all right. That was the hardest thing. Pretending everything was cool.

I spent so much time wondering what people expected me to do or say, I was exhausted by the end of the day. I'd go to bed, and feel like I could sleep forever.

I kind of liked Jamie though. He was friendly — he'd usually sit next to me in the classes we had together, and talk to me at lunch time and stuff. Sometimes I thought he might be — well — interested, you know? I hoped he wasn't. I have this way of deciding whether I'm interested. I imagine kissing them. And no matter how much I might like a guy, I usually end up thinking 'Yuk'. I've found that's a pretty good indication. And when I thought about kissing Jamie, that's pretty much what I thought.

Anyway, that was kind of the state of the nation when I did something really, really dumb. Doubly dumb, because by then I'd worked out it was definitely *not* the kind of thing you did — not if you wanted to be cool. Which I did.

It was in English, and we were talking about *The Merchant of Venice*, and Ms Henderson asked us who the hero of the play was. There was the usual space while everyone waited for someone else to say something, and then a few people muttered, 'Antonio'.

'Antonio. Does everyone agree with that?'

There was another space, then I said, 'No.'

Heads turned, I can tell you. I knew even then I'd really put my foot in it, but I have to tell you, *The Merchant of Venice* is one of my favourite stories. I can get very hot under the collar about things that are important to me.

So then, of course, Ms Henderson goes, 'And why would you disagree with that, Kate?'

So off I went. Full steam ahead at my most smartarse. Yes, I even quoted from the play. Without opening my book. Even now, when it's all over, I still get kind of hot and uncomfortable thinking about it. Anyway, Ms Henderson nodded, and tapped her cheek with her pen, and finally said, 'That's very perceptive, Kate.'

I think it was then I really realised what I'd done. Someone behind me muttered, 'That's very perceptive, Kate' — really sarcastic. Someone else made some smart comment about the colour of my face, of course. If the lights had been switched off, it must have lit up the whole room.

Ms Henderson tried to get me to say more, but I wouldn't. I guess I hoped that by shrugging my shoulders and acting dumb for the rest of the class I might make up for being a complete and utter jerk. No way.

'I never realised you were so — perceptive,' Lucy said as we left the room. Thanks very much, Loose, I thought. I just gave her this wimpy smile and made a run for it.

Now I was *really* miserable. My credibility — whatever there was of it — was shot to pieces. And at least before when I got home, all I wanted to do was go to bed and got to sleep and forget about it. Now I couldn't even do that. I just kept going over and over it in my mind, feeling worse and worse every time. I must've slept for two hours at most that night — and when I did sleep I had nightmares.

The next day I just tried to avoid everyone. I tried to avoid even looking at them. But at lunch time Jamie cornered me.

'Careful,' I said to him. 'You don't want to ruin your reputation by being seen with the smartarse of the century.'

He just laughed. 'I can handle the shame.'

'Don't forget the humiliation.'

'The scorn.'

'Ridicule.'

'Loneliness.'

'And missing out on Lucy's party!'

'Now that I *can* handle!'

We both laughed.

'That's better,' he said. 'You don't want to take it too seriously, you know.'

'I know. But it's one thing to know something …'

And another thing not to wish you were dead.

I didn't say it. Sometimes — most of the time — it's just impossible to say how you really feel. But Jamie knew what I meant.

'You shouldn't worry about being smart,' he said. 'I wish I was.'

Now I really didn't know what to say. Not that Jamie was a dunce. But from what I'd seen of him in class he wasn't exactly a straight-A student either. We sort of let that one slide.

'But how did you know all that stuff in the first place?'

'Just the way I grew up, I guess,'

'Which was ...?'

I looked at him for a bit. It was probably safe to tell him.

'When I was about ten or eleven ...' I started. Was that enough of an explanation? I went back a bit further. 'The place we used to live in ...'

I balked again.

Jamie laughed. 'Just pretend you're in English again,' he said.

I didn't mind him saying that. Somehow it made it better to be reminded of it in a joking way. I tried again.

'My dad's a mining engineer, and we've always lived in the bush. The last place we lived was a copper mine in the middle of the desert — have you ever heard of Woomera?'

He shook his head.

'It's in the middle of South Australia. The Americans kind of own it, and fire off rockets from there. And about fifty kilometres outside that is the place I used to live. Just a couple of dirt roads and a hole in the ground. There was never much to do there — the American kids stuck to themselves, no TV, no beach, no cafes, no anything. Once a month a couple of movies were flown in from Adelaide. That was about it. So I used to read a lot.'

'But nobody reads Shakespeare any more do they?'

I just looked at him.

'Sorry. So you read a lot.'

'I read a lot. And one day, when I was about ten or eleven, Dad discovered me reading James Bond books — which was a bit of a no-no, on account of the s-e-x in them.'

'So he made you read Shakespeare to improve your mind?'

'No! He asked me if I could understand it — which I could — and he said if I was still interested, when I was a bit older he'd let me read Shakespeare. Like it was even better than James Bond — something *really* grown-up. I couldn't wait. Well, the next birthday he gave me a complete set of Shakespeare, and sort of helped me through one of the plays — *Twelfth Night*, it was — explained the jokes to me — even the dirty ones.'

'Does Shakespeare tell dirty jokes?'

'Oh yeah! "Bawdy", my dad says.'

Jamie was looking a bit stunned. I think he was having trouble with the idea that anyone could actually *read* Shakespeare — let alone laugh at the jokes.

'Anyway, that's about that.'

We just sat there for a minute.

'You know,' Jamie said finally, 'You shouldn't worry too much. About being smart, I mean, or being cool. I'd rather be smart than cool any day.'

'I'd kind of like to be both.'

He just laughed. 'I mean — how much longer have you got here? Not even a year. And then, no one's going to care how cool you were in high school. It's what you know and what you can do that'll make the difference.'

'Now you sound like my mother!'

I got a really dirty look for that.

'And it's not as if you're a complete dag,' he went on.

'Just a semi-dag, huh?'

'Just a semi-dag,' he agreed.

I hit him — but not too hard. Jamie was all right. And I did feel much better.

So I tried not to let it worry me too much. One bad thing was, every time I went into English now, Ms Henderson gave me this glowing look, and spent the whole time talking to me instead of the rest of the class. It didn't make things any easier. I tried not to say too much, but it's kind of hard. I'd always really liked English — it would've been good to be able to talk about things, instead of sitting there like a complete dodo. Sometimes I felt like I was going to burst.

About a week later, we got this assignment in English. We were talking about script-writing, and we had to choose a television program, and write the script for one of the episodes. Then the next week, we were going to have some readings in class. This made me kind of anxious. The last thing I needed right now was to make a spectacle of myself again. I thought about writing something really bad — I figured if I made it the worst one in the class, I wouldn't have to read. This seemed like a sensible plan. Until I started writing it. Then I got a bit carried away. I chose 'Neighbours', and it was just so much fun making everyone do all these dumb things, and say really silly lines — though not much dumber or sillier than the things that happened most nights — I forgot all about The Plan, and just had a good time. In fact, I forgot all about the readings, too. Until ...

'Well, everyone, I must say I was very impressed with the standard of your scripts. I'm quite looking forward to hearing some of them today — and I'm sure you all are too. I'll give them all back first, then I've chosen four of you to read your work aloud. I think you'll enjoy hearing what the others have done — maybe after the class you might like to swap scripts, and have a read of a few more.'

Sure! Sometimes you wonder how teachers got to be teachers, they're so dumb.

Anyway, it looked like there was no escaping now. I got my script back — A+. Henderson had practically dribbled on the page she'd got so excited. My heart started pounding, and I could feel my face warming up already. I wondered if I should pretend to faint or something, but I wasn't sure I wouldn't look just as much of an idiot. So I just sat there.

The first name she called wasn't mine — it was Jamie's. I was a bit surprised, but he'd done this one on the news that was pretty good. The next one wasn't mine either (one of the Studiers) — or the next one. I was justing starting to relax when Henderson finally said, 'Now, Kate — let's hear yours.'

Someone in the back of the class groaned. Definitely groaned. Lucy leaned over.

'Have you got a nice BBC drama for us, Kate? Something perceptive?'

I ignored her. Sometimes it was all you *could* do with Loose. I just started reading instead.

My voice was a bit croaky to start with, but — believe it or not — into about the second page I got a couple of laughs. Everyone seemed to really like it. In fact, once everyone else started laughing, I had a bit of trouble keeping a straight face myself. Even Henderson cracked a smile.

When I'd finished, I actually got a round of applause. Jamie gave me a hug (sometimes he really did remind me of my mother!) — and even Lucy looked like she might be ready to recognise my existence again. Not that she'd laughed — but she'd actually smiled a couple of times. I'd seen it with my own eyes.

Outside the class, Jamie put his arm round my shoulders and gave me another hug. 'I told you it was okay to be smart.'

I just smiled. I felt pretty good.

Chapter 3

I wouldn't say it was a miracle, exactly. But that English class sure made a difference to my status. Lucy wasn't too happy that I'd put on such a good show — she didn't get to read hers at all — but it looked like she'd decided that I wasn't a complete dag after all.

Just a semi-dag.

The main thing that came out of it was that Lucy cornered me at the lockers the next day.

'Hi,' she said.

'Hi,' I said. I felt a bit nervous. Sometimes when Lucy smiles and says Hi and walks towards you, you feel like the next thing she's going to do is slap your face or something. She's never actually done this in the whole time I've known her, but sometimes you can't help feeling it just the same.

Anyway, she didn't slap me. Instead she goes — very casual — 'Are you doing anything Saturday night?'

'I don't have anything lined up yet,' I said.

I'd learned already that you never say 'no' when someone asks you if you're doing anything Saturday night. You say 'not yet' or 'nothing special' or something like that. Only complete dags admit to doing nothing on the weekend.

'How'd you like to come to the party at my place then?'

I shrugged. 'Sure.'

'It's at nine. My folks are away for the weekend. It'll be good.' I nodded.

'I'll write down the address for you in Legal later.'

'Great.'

Jamie had his head in his locker, and he was kind of shaking. I knew he was laughing, but Loose didn't seem to notice.

'Okay. I'll see you later then,' she said.

'Sure.' I smiled, and she walked off. As soon as she was down the corridor a bit I whacked Jamie on the bum.

'What's so funny!'

Jamie pulled his head out of the locker. His face and eyes were all red — he was laughing so much he was crying. He put his hand on my shoulder.

'You're so — cool!' he said admiringly.

I thumped him again. 'You just mind your manners, Mr Hamilton, or I won't invite you to *my* party!'

He laughed even more at that, and we went off to get some lunch.

So — I was going to Lucy's party. You know, sometimes it seems you just can't win. A week ago I would've been over the moon if I'd got an invite to Lucy's place. Now the thought of it was giving me nightmares. A party! What did you actually *do* at parties? From the things Lucy said, it sounded like you just drank and took drugs until you were sick. Sometimes on the ones in the movies, people stood around talking. In others there was dancing. I wasn't all that sure I *could* dance. I'd never tried — and Lucy's party probably wasn't a real good place to start, either. I wished there was someone I could ask for advice but there wasn't really. I couldn't ask Mum or Dad — I hadn't actually told them about it yet — and besides, what would they know? I thought about asking Jamie, but I didn't think I could tell even him that I'd *never* been to a party.

In the end I got the chance to sort of meet him halfway. He actually came up to me one lunch time later in the week, and asked if something was on my mind.

24

'No, no, nothing — really.'

He made me sit down. 'Come on, Kate. Tell mother.'

This was our joke — him being like my Mum. Could I tell him? I gave him a sort of squinty look, and took a deep breath.

'It's just — well, nothing really. It's just Lucy's party.'

'What about it?'

'She's a bit scary, you know.'

'What's she going to do? Bite your head off?'

I sort of smiled — though it wasn't really a laughing matter. It was hard to explain though.

'Lucy's no different to everyone else, you know. Well, she sort of is, but she's not dangerous. You've got nothing to worry about.'

'It's not that I'm worried about Lucy, really. It's just that — ' What could I say? 'It's just that I'm not really sure what to wear.'

I put on my hayseed voice. 'Things sure are different in this here big smoke, sonny.'

Jamie seemed to swallow that all right.

'Well, don't panic,' he said. 'If you like I'll come over after school tonight and check out your wardrobe.'

I gave him a hug. 'Thanks. That'd be nice.'

So that afternoon Jamie got a lift home from school with me and Mum. I'd had to tell him that my parents didn't know about the party yet, so he volunteered to break the news, and ask if I could go with him. I thought they might feel better about it if I was going with someone, instead of just wandering off into the night alone. I was right. Mum didn't say much, but I could tell she was pleased to think I had a boyfriend. She couldn't wait for Dad to get home to tell him the good news — and I couldn't wait for Jamie to leave so I could tell her the bad news. That Jamie wasn't my boyfriend, and never would be.

Anyway, I decided not to worry about that just now. I had other problems — and they turned out to be pretty big ones, too. I took Jamie down to my room and showed him where I kept my clothes. He looked through them for a while — every now and then he'd take something out and hold it up and look at it and go 'Mmm'. Then he'd put it away again.

Finally he said, 'That's it, is it?'

'Uh-huh.'

'Mmm.'

'Thanks! It's nice to know I'm the worst-dressed girl in Melbourne!'

'Oh, not *the* worst dressed!' He grinned at me. 'You're just such a — semi-dag!'

I flopped down on the bed. 'Great. I'm so glad you said you'd help me out.'

'I will! You'll just have to buy something on Saturday.'

'Sure!' I emptied my purse onto the bed. 'With eleven dollars and seventy-six cents?'

'Why not?'

'What am I going to buy with ten bucks? A new hanky?'

He laughed. 'Trust mother. If you'll get up early on Saturday moring, I guarantee we'll find you something to wear. But I have to play basketball at eleven, so I want you ready at nine.'

'With eleven dollars and seventy-six cents?'

'Guaranteed. Deal?'

'If you say so.' We shook on it. 'Deal.'

Just then Mum stuck her head round the door. 'Jamie, would you like to stay and have some dinner with us?'

I rolled my eyes. My folks seemed to get it all wrong. Even if Jamie *was* my boyfriend, I thought I was supposed to be the one who had to convince them he was a nice guy. Instead, she's asking him to dinner when she doesn't even know anything about him. Jamie didn't seem to mind her being so pushy, though.

'Sure — I'll just have to call home.'

'Of course. I'll show you where the phone is.'

Things had gone just about far enough. I butted in.

'It's in the lounge-room where we came in, near the fire. Mum, can I have a word with you?'

She gave me her 'amused' look, but said, 'Of course,' — and Jamie went off to find the phone.

Mum sat down on the bed next to me, still looking 'amused.'

'Well?'

'Mum, what are you doing?'

She swapped the 'amused' look for her 'innocent' look — the one she puts on when she's been through my room while I've been out and thrown away all my best junk.

'There's something I want to get straight right now,'I began. There's no point beating about the bush with parents. You learn pretty quickly that they just can't take a hint.

'Jamie is *not* my boyfriend. He's just a friend. I don't want you and Dad asking him what his prospects are or whether he'd like a big family, all right? He's just a friend, and he's helping me choose something to wear to Lucy's on Saturday. Absolutely nothing else.'

Mum held up her hands. 'Okay! My lips are sealed!' She got up and headed for the door.

'And, Mum?'

'Mmmm?'

'That means no telling Dad he's my boyfriend either.'

She smiled at me. 'Of course,' she said, and shut the door.

But I still couldn't relax. You just can't trust parents sometimes.

Anyway, Jamie stayed for dinner, and everything was okay, really. Mum and Dad did ask him a lot of questions about the party — what went on and who was going to be there and stuff. In a way I was glad — it gave me a bit of inside info, too. And no one embarrassed me too much, except when Dad started going on about how he'd like to drive me to Lucy's place and pick me up again at midnight. But Jamie suggested he'd come by and pick me up, and drop me home later in a taxi — and Mum said she'd pay for both our fares, which was nice. So all in all it turned out to be not too bad a night, and when I went to bed I felt better than I had in ages. In fact, for the first time since I started school, I went to bed feeling good.

And on Saturday, Jamie came through. He took me to this daggy shop in Hampton Street, where everything was second hand. As far as I knew it was where you took your old clothes — not where you went for new ones. But Jamie — again like Mum — was right. (Don't you hate it!) I came home with a fantastic dress — and some change!

There was even time for me to go home and try it on with shoes and a bit of make-up. I was kind of nervous, actually, when I came out of the bathroom. Jamie stood back and folded his arms and sort of looked at me for a minute. Then he said, 'You look great.'

I raced down to the bedroom to check myself out in the mirror. He was right again. I did!

I went with him to the gate.

'Thanks,' I said. 'I do look good, don't I?'

'Miss Modesty!'

'Don't I?' (I had to be sure.)

'You look good.'

He got halfway out the gate, then couldn't help saying, 'For a semi-dag.'

Chapter 4

Mum and Dad, who'd been out in the garden during the fashion show that morning, were pretty amazed when I appeared after dinner in my party gear. I thought Dad might say something — he looked like he was going to — but he just laughed instead. Which wasn't great, but it was better than being told to go and change. And Mum said I looked very nice. To tell you the truth, what I felt was very sick.

And Jamie wasn't much help.

'Hello, dag,' he said when he arrived.

I just swallowed. This was no time for dumb jokes.

'You right to go?'

I nodded, and followed him outside.

'Dress looks great.'

'Thanks.'

My voice sounded like I'd just swallowed a packet of nails. He looked kind of surprised.

'You feeling all right?'

I nodded again, and kind of stretched my lips out. It was supposed to be a smile. He just looked at me again, and then gave my hand a squeeze.

'You're funny, aren't you? There's nothing to worry about.'

I didn't say anything. A minute later he said, 'Did you bring anything to drink?'

'No,' I croaked.

'Do you drink?'

'I drink wine at home sometimes.'

'We'll stop and buy you some wine then. You look like you could use it.'

I wasn't sure that getting smashed was going to make the evening a big success, but I bought a half-bottle of red wine and stuffed it into the pocket of my coat. Having a bottle in a brown paper bag in my pocket made me feel like a bit of a dero, but I figured I could always throw it in the bin when I arrived if I had to.

About ten seconds later (it seemed like ten seconds, anyway) we were outside Lucy's place — and I felt pretty much like I had the first day at school. I grabbed Jamie's coat.

I didn't say anything, but he kind of read my mind, and laughed at me.

'Don't worry. I'll look after you.'

And we went inside.

Well, it looked pretty terrifying to me. It was dark, and the music was so loud it made my eardrums vibrate. Basically, it looked like a whole lot of Very Cool strangers shouting at each other.

Give me that wine!' Jamie bellowed in my ear. I handed it over, and he disappeared. My heart was thumping along with the music — just about as loudly, too. I was ready to turn around and run all the way home when Jamie reappeared with a plastic cup half full of red wine.

I took a sip and shouted, 'Is it time to go yet?'

He laughed, but said, 'Katie, get a grip on yourself! Just imagine it's lunch time at school.'

And he grabbed my hand and dragged me into the middle of the room.

Well, it wasn't bad advice. By this time my eyes had got used to the dark, and I recognised quite a few people from school. There were still a lot of strangers — and even the people I did know looked really different all dressed up. But luckily, since that English class, most of the people I did know didn't mind talking to me, so it wasn't so bad. I never did have much to say to anyone at lunch time at school, and the music made it kind of hard to have a conversation, but I struggled along okay, mainly smiling and nodding and pretending to sip my drink.

Then Jamie popped up again, leading a girl by the arm.

'Katie, this is Suzanne, my next door neighbour. Suzy, this is Kate, that I told you about!'

'Hi!' I yelled, wondering exactly what Jamie had told her. She smiled at me and nodded and looked pretty friendly, so it can't have been too bad.

I'd just opened my mouth to say something when someone grabbed my arm and swung me around. It was Lucy.

'Hi!' she shrieked. She really stank, and looked a bit wobbly. I don't know what she'd been drinking, or how much, but it smelt awful. And her hair was a mess.

'Hi,' I said, trying to breathe through my mouth.

'You look great! Really! I'm so glad you came! Kate, this is my boyfriend, John!'

She had this bloke by the hand. He was looking pretty bored, and pretty bleary too. I stared at him a bit. He was good-looking, but sort of ugly too. Like he spent his whole life thinking of horrible things to do to people.

'Hi,' I said again, and wished they'd both go

away.

'You look so good! Great dress! Really!' Loose said again, and then kind of staggered off into the crowd. I took a big breath. The air was still full of cigarette smoke and about twenty different kinds of perfume, but at least it was better than her breath. The girl Suzy was still standing next to me, and laughing.

'Fabulous frock!' she shouted. 'Really!'

I laughed too.

And then we stood there, kind of looking at each other. I liked the look of Suzy — and she obviously had a sense of humour. I really wanted to say something witty and fascinating and get a conversation going, but my mind was a total blank. And then, while I was standing there trying to think of something to say, and wondering if I looked like a complete idiot, Suzy said something to me. Only I was so busy being worried, I missed it.

'What?' I shouted.

'I just asked — are you a friend of Lucy's?'

Was I a friend of Lucy's? I didn't know what to say. I kind of opened my mouth and made some noises, but nothing that actually made any sense. And then we stood there for a bit longer, with me feeling more and more like an idiot. And finally Suzy saw one of her friends, and smiled at me, and walked off.

I didn't know whether to be sorry or glad.

It seemed like about twenty-four hours later that Jamie finally rescued me.

'There you are! I thought you must've run off.'

'Just hiding.'

'Well it's time to go. We promised your dad.'

Sounded fine to me. 'I'll go and get my coat.'

I ducked into Lucy's bedroom.

When I came out again, Jamie was already outside.

I thought about going and saying goodbye to Lucy, but I didn't want to catch her vomiting into the azaleas, so I let it go. I just made for the door as quickly as I could. So quickly that I smashed straight into someone who was coming out of the bathroom.

'Careful!' He grabbed hold of my arms. I looked up and nearly died. It was *the* most gorgeous guy I'd ever seen in my life. Really. He must have been about six foot tall, with curly blond hair, and just the most beautiful blue eyes. I kind of choked. He was looking down, laughing at me. My face must have looked like a boiled tomato. He opened his mouth to say something, but I didn't want to hear it. I had to get out of there.

'Sorry!' I said, and ran for my life.

Jamie was standing outside by the taxi.

'Hello! What's up?'

'Nothing!' I took a couple of breaths. 'Really.'

He stared at me for a bit, then opened the car door. 'In you get then.'

We didn't talk much on the way home though Jamie looked at me a couple of times. I was really tired — so was he, I think.

'Thanks for looking after me,' I said, and yawned. He had his eyes shut, but he patted me on the head.

'Any time, Katie. See you Monday.'

'Yeah. Bye.'

I went into the house and flopped into bed. I was *never* going to another party as long as I lived.

When I woke up the next morning, the wind was blowing the curtains away from the window, and I could see it was a beautiful day. In the kitchen Mum and Dad were making coffee, the radio was going, and cat was asking for her breakfast. Ten o'clock and all's well. I rolled over onto my side and thought about last night. Jamie had been good — he'd tried — but it'd still been pretty awful. Suzy had been nice. I wish I hadn't been such an idiot — she looked like someone I would have liked to have got to know. But I'd blown that.

And then there was that guy I'd run into. I

rolled over onto my other side and curled up a bit tighter. He was gorgeous. No doubt about it. Just thinking about it made me feel — what? Hard to say. Sort of good and bad at the same time. And I'd been such a jerk! As usual. Thinking about that made me jump out of bed and pull some clothes on. Time to stop thinking and have some breakfast!

Mum and Dad were eating their muesli, but both of them stopped and put down their spoons and looked up at me when I walked in. I covered my face with my hands.

'Oh no! The inquisition!'

They both laughed and Mum got up to pour me some orange juice. Dad made the first move.

'Did you have a good time?'

'Yeah. I had a pretty good time,' I lied.

'Jamie took good care of you?' This was Mum.

'Yep. He was good.'

'Was there — uh — alcohol there, Katie?' Dad, pretending not to be too interested. I couldn't help smiling. Sometimes they were just so predictable! I decided I might as well be honest.

'Yep. Lucy — it was her party, you know — was really revolting. It's enough to put you off drinking for life.'

'Mmm?' Dad just raised his eyebrows at me.

'I had a glass of wine.'

'You certainly don't look hung-over.'

'Well I'm not!'

'All right, dear. We weren't doubting you.' Mum gave me my orange juice.

'Did you meet any nice people?'

'Mmm,' I said. What else could I say?

'That's nice.' Mum settled herself in her chair and picked up her spoon again.

I almost told them about the guy I'd run into. I don't know why. It wasn't even as if there was anything to tell. I just felt like if I didn't mention it I was going to burst. Instead I finished my breakfast and then rang up Jamie.

'Hi, it's Kate.'

'Hi. Sleep well?'

'Yep. How about you?'

'Yeah, fine.'

I wasn't sure what to say next. 'Um — thanks for taking me last night.'

'I told you, don't mention it.'

'No, well, I appreciate it.'

'That's okay.'

More silence.

'Uh — Kate — I don't mean to be rude, but did you call me for a reason?'

'Sort of.' How embarrassing! Still, I knew if I didn't say anything, I'd regret it. I had to find out who that guy was.

'Did you know everyone at the party last night?'

'Yeah, mostly, I think. It was the usual crowd.'

'How about a tall guy with blond hair and blue eyes?'

'Well, there were a couple. Do you mean the bloke with Julie Crawford?'

'No — a really gorgeous guy, with curly hair — in a white T-shirt.'

'Curly, not wavy?'

'Yeah.'

'That'd be Pete Shardlow. He's Lucy's cousin, goes to the tech next door to the tennis courts.'

'Oh.' It wasn't exactly the best news I could've had. 'Thanks.'

'Why'd you want to know?'

'Oh — no reason.'

'Kate!'

'Really — it's nothing. I just saw him and wondered — you know — who he was.'

'Mmm. Well, don't get your hopes up, Katie.'

'Why?'

'I don't think he's exactly your type.'

'How do you know what my type is?'

'Well, I know what you're like, and I know what he's like, that's all.'

'Anyway, it's beside the point. It doesn't matter

if he's my type or not.'

'Sure.'

'And you don't have to say 'sure' like that either, Jamie Hamilton!'

He laughed. 'See you Monday, Katie.'

'Yeah. See you then.'

I hung up.

Chapter 5

Lucy's cousin! Great! *The* most gorgeous guy in the world, and he had to be a horrible thug from the tech, related to the most terrifying girl in school.

Not that it mattered. He must've been able to tell at one look that I was a complete dork. And I'd probably never even see him again anyway. So even if he wasn't a horrible thug, there was absolutely no point even thinking about him.

Fine. So why couldn't I stop thinking about him?

On Monday Jamie tried again to get me to tell him why I wanted to know about Peter Shardlow. What could I say? Nothing. Which is exactly what Jamie got out of me.

It was weird seeing Lucy in her school

uniform, looking pretty much as stunning and normal as she usually did. I wouldn't forget what she was like on Saturday in a hurry. I was sort of embarrassed to look at her, and there's no way in the world I would've mentioned the party — but she was the one who asked me if I'd had a good time.

'Yeah, thanks.'

'Me too,' she said, and went off to her next class.

I just looked at her. There were obviously some things I was *never* going to understand, no matter how long I lived in the city.

I spent most of the week trying to forget about Saturday night, but it wasn't easy. When I wasn't cringing about making a fool of myself, I was thinking about — you know — Him. Wondering what he was like, and where he lived, and the things he liked to do, and just remembering the way he looked and the way he'd smiled at me, and his beautiful eyes, and wondering if his hair was really as soft as it looked.

Pretty revolting, really.

Saturday morning I couldn't face the thought of sitting around the house all day — and I certainly wasn't going to do any homework. So I decided to go back to the shop Jamie had taken me to and poke around in there for an hour or so.

I'd just turned the corner into the street where the shop was when I saw this group of guys walking toward me. They were all wearing jeans and T-shirts, and a few of them had tatts. I kept my eyes on the footpath, and was just thinking about crossing the street to get out of their way when one of them said, 'Hey!'

I've never wanted to be invisible so much in my life. I was terrified. I pretended not to hear — if there hadn't been so much traffic I would've run across the street. But there was no escape, so I kept my head down and tried to walk past them. One of the guys reached out and touched my arm.

'Hey — didn't I see you on Saturday night?'

I looked up. I swear to God my heart stopped beating — and then started again like it was about to burst. It was *him* — and he was smiling at me. He still had hold of my arm, and he called out to his mates, 'See you there, guys!'

Then he looked back down at me.

'You're the one who crashed into me at Lucy McGregor's party — you ran off before I could ask your name. I haven't seen you around before, have I?'

'No,' I managed to say. I even tried to smile — which isn't easy when you're on the point of collapsing. 'I only came down to Melbourne a couple of months ago.'

'Uh-huh. So what *is* your name?'

'Kate. Kate Anderson.'

'Kate.' He seemed pretty pleased with that. 'I'm Pete Shardlow.'

I almost said, 'I know', but stopped myself just in time. Instead I just said, 'Hi.'

'Do you live near here?'

'Yeah, in Bridge Street.'

'Near the park?'

'Uh-huh — just across the road.'

'Maybe I could come by and see you some time?'

I had to be dreaming! The most gorgeous guy on the planet — possibly in the entire universe — just asked if he could come by and see me some time. I was really smiling now. I seemed to have lost control of my facial muscles.

'That'd be nice.'

'So what's your address? And maybe you'd better tell me your phone number, so I can call first to make sure it's okay. Am I going too fast? Do you like pushy guys?'

I had to laugh. 'Sure I do.'

'Do you have a pen and paper?'

'No — do you?'

'Oh, I always carry a note book and pen with me, for writing down ideas for my novel.'

I almost believed him. I almost said 'do you?' — and he knew it. He laughed and took hold of my arm again. I liked it when he touched me. It wasn't sleazy. It was just nice and friendly. 'Come on then.'

We went up the street and into a newsagent, and he bought a pen and some paper. Just to write down my phone number. I was sure I'd died and gone to heaven. That was it. The thugs had actually attacked me and knifed me and I'd died — and now I was in heaven. Well, I didn't care. As long as it didn't end.

'Well, Kate,' he goes, like he really liked saying my name. 'Ah — maybe I could call you a bit later in the week — maybe I could see you sometime on the weekend?'

I could hardly speak. I was sure I was grinning like an idiot. I nodded and swallowed and managed to say, 'That'd be nice.'

He laughed at me. I must've been looking pretty confused.

'You sure are a cute little thing, Kate Anderson. I've been thinking that all week. Except I didn't know you were Kate Anderson, of course — but you know what I mean.' Was he serious? I just kept on smiling. 'Well, I'll call you during the week, okay?'

'Okay,' I managed.

He stood there for a minute, then just waved and walked off. I was still glued to the footpath, staring after him. I couldn't believe it. It just couldn't be true. Before, when guys had asked me out, they'd always been people I knew really well — dumb American guys at Woomera that none of the cool American girls would have anything to do with. They'd sort of hang around for weeks, trying to be friendly, and then ask you to do something you'd never want to do in a million years, even if they weren't the biggest dags in school. No one like Pete Shardlow had ever even spoken to me, let alone just walked up to me in the street and asked me out! Me! He didn't even know me! It was so weird. I started to feel a bit panicky. I hadn't imagined it, had I?

I walked back home in a kind of daze, going over every single thing we'd said to each other — trying to find the catch. In fact — this is how blown out I was — when I got home, I snuck into the bathroom and took my own temperature, just to make sure I wasn't delirious. My heart was beating fast, but I wasn't sick. It was true. Pete Shardlow, thug, man in a million, had walked up to a nobody in the street and asked her out. Asked me out! Well, sort of. Asked to ask me out. Which is pretty polite, really, for a thug. I had to go and lie down. It was all too much.

47

'Katie? Are you all right, sweetheart?' Mum came in and switched on the lamp by the bed. I was sure she'd be able to tell that Something Incredible had happened to me, but after squinting at me for a minute, she just said, 'Dinner's ready, love. Do you want to get up now?'

'Sure.' I sat up on the edge of the bed.

'You feeling okay?'

'Yeah, I feel fine. I was just a bit tired.'

'Well, I'm about to serve up.'

'Okay. I'll be there in a sec.'

All through dinner I was wondering if I should say something. I didn't know what, exactly, but about ten times I opened my mouth to say 'Guess what?', then shut it again. I'd wait until he actually called before breaking the news. But I could hardly sit still in my chair, let alone swallow my food. Mum and Dad tried to get a conversation going, but I wasn't much help, so in the end they gave up and talked to each other. They were pretty used to me being off in a world of my own.

I went to bed early, mainly because all I really wanted to do was lie in the dark and think about it all. I'd thought I'd never get to sleep, but I guess I must have, because the next thing I knew the next door neighbours had started up their lawn mower, and Dad was making coffee in the kitchen. It seemed weird that everything should be exactly the same, when my whole life had changed forever, but there it is. Lawns still have to be mowed, I guess.

I poured myself a cup of coffee and sat down at the table.

'What are your plans for today, sweetheart?'

I shrugged. 'Hadn't really thought about it. Might read a bit. Might take Cass down to the beach.' Casanova was our dalmation. When he was a pup he had some pretty weird habits, but he seemed to have grown out of them.

'If you've got time, your mother and I could use some help out the back. We're pulling down that shed today.'

'Sure.' It was a great day outside, and even though I knew it was really un-cool, I kind of liked doing things with my parents sometimes. They were pretty good fun — for parents.

So after breakfast I put on my grottiest jeans and T-shirt, and a pair of Mum's gardening gloves, and grabbed a crowbar. There's something really good about totally wrecking something. It was filthy, though. Every time you pulled off a bit of tin, this huge cloud of dirt came with it. That shed must've been standing there for about a hundred years. Around the middle

49

of the morning the doorbell rang. Mum and Dad were pulling off the roof.

'Would you see who that is, Katie?'

Still with the cobweb-covered crowbar in my hand, I went round the side of the house to the front door.

'You're really an axe murderer!'

It was him.

Chapter 6

It was him, standing there as gorgeous as ever, at my front door. And there was me — looking like I'd just crawled out of the slime pit. What did cool people do? Did they duck under the shower and freshen their make-up every time the doorbell rang? Or maybe they just never did things like pull down old garden sheds. They were too busy being glamorous and popular. I don't know why these things always happened to me.

Still, what could I do?

'Hi! I — uh — wasn't expecting you.'

He was trying really hard not to laugh. 'I can tell. Do you want me to go away? You look kind of busy — not to mention dangerous!'

'No — not unless I've scared you off!'

'It takes more than a five-foot axe murderer to scare me off. What are you up to?'

'Pulling down the shed out the back, with Mum and Dad.'

'Well, I guess this is my big chance to meet them.'

I couldn't believe it. I thought thugs were supposed to be — well — different. Thuggish. They certainly weren't supposed to be nice. But Pete Shardlow sure was a nice guy.

'I might just go and have a bit of a wash.'

'Don't bother,' he said, taking hold of my arm. 'You look just fine.'

So we went round to the back of the house. Mum was down off the roof, but Dad was still up there, chucking down bits of wood and tin.

'You sure have a violent family,' Pete whispered as we came round the side of the house. I just gave him a look.

'Ah — Mum — Dad . . . ' I had to talk kind of loud to get their attention. They both looked really surprised when they saw I had someone with me. Dad let himself down from the roof.

'Ah — this is Pete Shardlow. He's . . . ' What? '. . . a friend of mine.' I hoped that didn't sound too dumb.

Dad took off his gloves and walked up to Pete. They shook hands.

'Hello, Pete.'

'Hi.'

Mum smiled and nodded and said hello. 'Would you like a cup of tea or coffee Pete?' she asked.

'I don't want to interrupt you ...'

'No, no, we were just about to take a break — come into the house while Katie and Dave wash.'

So we all trooped into the house — Dad and I went off to the bathroom, Mum put the kettle on and washed her hands at the sink. By the time I got back, they were chatting away like they'd known each other for years. Dad came back as Mum was pouring the coffee.

'So how did you two meet?' he asked.

Dad likes to get to the point. But at least he didn't say 'So what do you want with my daughter?' or something like that.

'At Lucy's party last weekend.'

'You didn't say anything about it, Kate.' Mum raised her eyebrows at me. I started to get a bit warm.

'Actually we really only met in the street yesterday. At the party Kate just ran straight into me, then ran straight off again in the other direction.'

'Mmm,' Mum said. 'Kate doesn't always notice where she's going ...'

'Or what she's doing ...'

'Or saying ...'

'Or eating ...'

'Or wearing ...'

'Or where she is ...'

'Or who she's with ...'

'Or who's talking to her ...'

Mum and Dad might've been having a good time. I sure wasn't.

'All right, all right! I'm not that bad!'

Mum and Dad just looked at each other. Sometimes I really wished they'd behave like normal people — you know, like parents were supposed to. Not like some comedy routine or something. Still, three out of the four people in the kitchen seemed to find it pretty funny. And at least Pete looked relaxed. In fact, it was hard to imagine him not relaxed. I couldn't help wondering — for the millionth time — why he was bothering with me. Still, who was I to argue with a gift from God?

Anyway, we drank our coffee and chatted for a while. At least, those three did most of the chatting, and I just sort of looked. They were carrying on like they'd known each other all their lives. It was a bit weird, but it was nice too. And I could have sat there all day, just looking at him and listening to him talk.

But Mum and Dad finally finished their coffee, and this horrible fruit bread they like to eat — each slice weighs about three kilos — and got up from the table.

'Well, we'd better get back to it. What do you want to do Katie?'

What did I want to do? Dance, sing, turn cartwheels, laugh like a maniac. But I guess that wasn't what they meant. While I was trying to think of something to say, Pete said, 'Maybe I could give you a hand out there.'

'Oh — you don't want to spend your Sunday wrestling with our shed, Pete ...'

Yes he does! Yes he does!

'Sure I would.'

'Well, we could certainly use an extra pair of hands. Would you like an old shirt to put on?'

'Yep, that'd be good.'

'Katie, why don't you go and find Pete an old shirt of your dad's.'

On the way down to Dad's room I said, 'You know, you don't have to stay. We could go down to the beach or into town or something.'

'No — I really would like to stay. I sort of like the idea of totally wrecking something.' He grinned at me. 'And I like seeing you all wild and filthy with cobwebs in your hair and the crowbar in your hand, too.'

This seemed pretty weird to me. I told him so.

'You always look so neat. It's fun seeing you completely haywire.'

'What do you mean "always" — you've only seen me twice?'

He leaned against the doorway into Mum and Dad's room. 'I guess so … But you just look like such a cute, neat little package … And there's something about you — I feel like I've known you a long time.'

I looked at him for a minute. He was just standing there smiling at me, and I couldn't help smiling back.

'That's nice,' I said, really softly. And it was.

I went and got him a shirt.

Well, we had a great time that afternoon. It was fun ripping into the old shed, getting totally filthy, going completely wild. After we'd pulled a whole lot of bits off we stomped on them and broke them into little bits, then carried them out to this big bin in the street. And sometimes there were gigantic man-eating spiders. This was our cue — Mum's and mine — to scream and run over to the edge of the yard. Then Dad or Pete would stomp over like cowboys and squish them, and we'd act very impressed and tell them how big and brave they were. It was fun.

We stopped in the middle of the day. Mum

and I made some of sandwiches and Dad and Pete poured the beer and we sat in the sun in the only clear space in the garden, feeling pretty good about the mess we'd made. By the end of the day the bin out the front was overflowing, and there was this big patch of dirt in the corner of the yard where the ugliest shed in the world used to be. We were all filthy and scratched and our muscles were aching (at least, mine were) — but we all felt good. Sometimes the strangest things are the best fun.

'Well, Pete, thanks for all your help. We really didn't think we'd get it all done today.' Dad peeled off his gloves and ruffled up his hair. Dust and rust and cobwells fell everywhere.

'Yes, Pete, thanks. You must come over and try some of the great vegies I'm going to grow there.'

Pete smiled, and looked at me then looked back at Mum. 'That'd be nice.'

'In fact, would you like to stay and have some dinner with us tonight? It seems the least we can do.'

I was really hoping he'd say yes, but he shook his head.

'Thanks very much, but I can't tonight. I'd better be getting home.'

'Well, perhaps another time. You might like to arrange something with Katie.'

'Yeah — Kate and I'll arrange something.' And he looked at me again, this little sideways, smiling look. I blushed.

'Well, I'm going to hit the shower.' Dad shook Pete's hand, and said thanks again, and went off into the house. The party was over.

I went round the side to the front of the house with Pete, and then sort of stood with my hands in my pockets. I smiled, and he smiled, and we just stood there for a minute. Finally he said, 'Do you want to walk up the street with me a little way?'

I smiled a bit more.

'Sure.'

So we walked on up the street a bit, and after a while he put his arm round my shoulders. It felt good — warm and strong — and I could feel his muscles against the back of my head. I rested my head against his shoulder a bit, and then after a while I put my arm around his waist. We didn't say anything. The sun was starting to set, and all the way down the street the big trees were starting to turn red and yellow. There was already a few leaves on the ground. It didn't matter that we were both sweaty and dirty, or that I hardly knew him, or that I was a daggy girl from the country who'd only been to one party in her whole life.

The street looked like the most beautiful street in the world, and I felt beautiful too. Not a bit daggy. Not even semi-daggy. And all the dirt and sweat just made Pete more gorgeous than ever. I snuck a little look at him, and he looked down at me and smiled. I snuggled back against his shoulder, and he gave me a bit of a squeeze and rubbed his check against the top of my head.

'Your hair's filthy,' he whispered.

'I know.' I felt pretty good about that too.

Then we were at the top of my street, where Pete turned off toward his place. We stopped, and he still didn't say anything. He just sort of turned around and put his other arm round me and hugged me really, really tightly. I was finding it a bit hard to breathe. I wasn't sure whether that was because he was about to break my ribs, or just because — well — you know. My heart was sure beating pretty fast, and I felt a bit dizzy. But where my ear was pressed against his chest I could hear his heart pounding away too, which was nice. It was exciting too. And then he loosened his grip on me a bit, and brushed my hair back from my face with one hand, and leant down and kissed me.

If I'd had time to think about it I probably would have panicked. But it was all so simple and easy, really. It just seemed like the natural thing to do. And it was wonderful, it was just the sweetest thing. His lips were very soft, and so was his face (except where it was a bit gritty). I felt like that was all I wanted to do for the rest of my life — stand on a street corner on a Sunday evening in autumn and kiss Peter Shardlow. And to tell you the truth, I don't think he would've minded too much either.

Of course, we had to stop sooner or later. But when we did, he just hugged me a bit tighter again, and I rested my face against his chest, and we stood like that for a while longer. Finally though, we realised it was getting pretty cold and dark, and we let each other go. Pete kept hold of my hand for a bit longer.

'I'll give you a call soon,' he said. His voice was a bit croaky. I gave his hand a little squeeze, then stood up on tiptoe and kissed him one last time.

'That'd be nice,' I whispered.

'See you then.'

'See you.'

And he walked off down the street.

I was really cold now — I still only had my T-shirt on, and it was pitch dark. My hair was full of dirt, and I ached all over, and I was starving.

But I didn't care.

I was in love.

Chapter 7

Dad was in the kitchen starting dinner by the time I got back in, and Mum was in the shower. You can tell when Mum's in the shower. She sort of whistles through her teeth, not really a tune, just these couple of watery notes that sounded like a tune to her. Funny about that. My mum's quite a good singer, but her whistling's really horrible.

Anyway, I went to sit in the kitchen till she was out of the bathroom. Dad looked up from chopping vegies.

'Pete lives in Perth, does he?'

'No, just in Sheridan Street,' I said. Dad just smiled and went on chopping up beans, and I realised what he meant. He looked up again and grinned at me, and I grinned back like an idiot.

But I wasn't about to say anything else.

'He's a nice bloke.'

'Mmm,' I said. What else could I say?

We were quiet for a bit, then Dad said, 'Your mother's out of the shower now.'

'Mmm,' I said again, and wandered off. What else could I say?

I felt like I was in a dream. Nothing seemed quite real. I tried to concentrate on regular things, but I couldn't stop thinking about standing on the coner of Bridge Street with Peter Shardlow's arms around me. It had kind of taken over my mind.

At lunch time on Monday Jamie found me sitting in the sun, daydreaming.

'Earth calling Katie, earth calling Katie...come in Katie...'

I laughed. 'Hi! How are you?'

'Good. What's with you?'

He looked at me for a minute with his eyebrows up. 'I mean why have you been wandering round all day looking like the cat that's swallowed the canary. And the cream, not to mention the casserole?'

'Oh well...'

'Mmm?'

'It's nothing really...' But I was dying to tell somebody.

'I can tell you're dying to tell somebody. You look about ready to burst.'

I was sometimes sure Jamie could read my mind.

Didn't I say he was like my mother?

'Well ... ' I said it again. Where should I start? 'You know how I asked you about that guy at the party?'

'Peter Shardlow?'

'Yeah.'

'What about it?'

'I met him down the street on Saturday.'

Jamie leaned back and kind of squinted at me. 'That's it.'

I shook my head.

'Well? Don't kill me with suspense!'

'He asked for my phone number. And address.'

Jamie made a funny kind of noise. 'Did he just.'

'Mmm.' I looked down at my shoes. We were quiet for a minute.

'Well, don't get your hopes up, Katie. Pete Shardlow's a — ah — popular kind of guy.'

I looked at my shoes a bit longer. 'He came round to my place on Sunday. He stayed for lunch and helped me and Mum and Dad pull down the garden shed.'

He made another funny sound. It sounded a lot like a laugh, but I couldn't be sure.

'Pete Shardlow came round and had lunch with you and your mum and dad?'

'Mmm.'

Lucy was just walking past, but this stopped her. 'What did you say about Pete?' she asked, looking at me kind of suspiciously. Jamie jumped in before I could say anything.

'He dropped by Katie's place on Sunday and had lunch with her and her mum and dad.'

It didn't sound that funny to me, but Lucy burst out laughing. 'You're kidding!'

'It's true!' I was getting a bit embarrassed. What was so funny?

'You must be joking. Peter Shardlow?'

I was getting pretty annoyed. 'What's so bloody funny about that?'

Lucy looked down at me, making her face serious. 'Nothing at all. That sounds perfectly reasonable to me.' She choked again, then reached down and patted my head. 'You just be careful, little Katie.'

Sometimes I really hated Lucy McGregor. I mean really. I was pretty angry — not just with her, but with Jamie too. I thought he was supposed to be my friend. In fact, I said to him, 'I thought you were supposed to be my friend.'

He stopped laughing — or at least stopped trying not to laugh, if you know what I mean. He gave me a hug.

'Sorry, Kate. It's just… it's just a bit out of the ordinary, that's all. I mean, it's all a bit sudden, isn't it?'

'So?'

'Well — nothing, I guess. But Lucy's right. Be careful, won't you.'

'Of what?'

I couldn't be sure, but I think he went a bit red in the face.

'I guess… it's just that… what I mean is — I may be wrong — but it just sometimes seems to me that there are some things you don't know very much about.'

Well, he was right. But that didn't mean I wanted to hear it. I was about to get really mad, but he gave me another hug.

'That's not bad, you know. You can't help not knowing things if you've never had a chance to learn them. I guess I just meant be careful how you — ah — find out about — the, ah, things you mightn't know much about. That's all.'

He looked so embarrassed, and — believe it or not — I did know what he meant. I stopped being angry.

'All right, mother. I promise I'll be careful.'

Thank goodness it was time for the next class.

I started to wish I'd never said anything to

Jamie. One minute I'd been feeling on top of the world — and now — well, if I wasn't exactly at the bottom, I certainly wasn't feeling too good about things.

As if just Peter wasn't enough to think about for the next hundred years or so, it looked like I'd have to sort out this sex business as well. I knew already that it was pretty un-cool to be a virgin. But from the way Jamie and Lucy had just been carrying on, it looked like it wasn't a real big secret that I was one. I could live with that. But what about Pete? Did he know? Did he care? What did he expect? What would I do if he asked? Or did guys even ask? Maybe I should think about self-defence lessons. Maybe I should never see him again. Maybe I shouldn't take self-defence lessons. (Now *that* was a mind-boggling thought.) I really just didn't know.

And then I had an even worse thought. What if I didn't get the chance? What if I didn't even get the chance to never see him again, or say yes or no, or fight him off or not. I thought about the way Lucy had laughed at me. Maybe he wasn't even really interested. Maybe maybe maybe. Maybe I should see a psychiatrist. Maybe I should just stop thinking about it.

Sure.

Well, I did my best not to think about it — which meant I ended up thinking about it only around ten times a day. Which wasn't too bad, considering. I concentrated on my homework, I concentrated on having conversations with my parents, I concentrated on behaving like a normal person at school — and in the middle of all that concentrating I probably only thought about Pete Shardlow maybe once every hour or so.

Luckily, before I completely wore myself out, the phone rang on Wednesday night, and it was for me. It was him. Dad called to me from the lounge-room — I was down in my bedroom Concentrating like crazy. But now that he'd actually called, I wasn't sure I wanted to talk to him. If I'd been able to hide in my bedroom from Sunday to Wednesday I would've been all right. I would have had nothing to think about but how wonderful everything was. But since talking with Jamie — and especially Lucy (who had been making silly, smart-arse comments all week) — I didn't feel so wonderful. And when I finally picked up the phone I almost expected him to breathe really heavily and say, 'How about it, baby?'

But he didn't. He just said, 'Hi, Katie.'

Well, that wasn't so bad. It meant I could say something pretty regular myself, like, 'Hi.' Which is what I did.

'How's your week been?'

Like a nightmare, I thought. 'Pretty good,' I said. 'How about you?'

'Oh, not so bad. Just an average week.'

'Mmm.'

We were quiet for a bit, then he laughed. 'It's funny, talking to you on the phone. It makes me think I don't know you at all. It's not like standing looking at you.'

I made a little sound. I didn't exactly know what to say.

'Not very chatty, are you?'

'Uh — no...' I was going really red. Thank God he couldn't see me.

There was some more silence, then he finally said, 'Look, you don't mind me calling, do you? I mean — I thought — did you want me to call?' He sounded kind of nervous. It gave me a little pain in my chest, but it felt good.

'I'm glad you called — really.'

'Would you like to do something on Saturday night, then?'

'Yes!'

'How'd you like to go to a film or something?'

'That'd be nice.' I liked films — and they were pretty safe, too.

'What sort of things do you like to see?'

'Well — just about anything. I like old films.'

'Uh huh.'

I sort of figured he didn't like old films too much. I tried again.

'I really like horror films too.'

'Do you really? Like horror films?'

'Yep.'

'Great. Well, let's do that then. Do you know what's on?'

'No, not really...'

'Well, why don't I bring a paper round on Saturday afternoon, and we can choose something then — if that's okay with you?'

'That sounds great.'

We went quiet again. Finally he — again — said, 'Okay then. I'll see you Saturday.'

'Okay.' I felt like I had to do something else — he'd been trying hard, and I hadn't been much help. So I said, 'And I really am glad you called.'

He didn't seem to mind that too much.

'That's good,' he said, really quietly. I loved the sound of his voice. I could listen to it for hours.

'Bye then,' he said.

'Bye.'

He hung up — but I couldn't bear to put the receiver down. I just sat there with it still against my ear, listening to it go 'beep beep beep.'

Chapter 8

After that I felt all right again for a couple of days. Pretty good, really. Well, all right, fantastic. He'd sounded so nice and normal on the phone — I couldn't believe the things Jamie and Lucy had been saying. Or hinting, anyway, How well did Jamie know him, anyway? Lucy probably knew him pretty well — he was her cousin, after all. But that didn't mean anything either. I wouldn't put it past her to be making it up — or at least exaggerating, just to scare me off. I could tell she wasn't too pleased that Pete was interested in me, though I don't know why. It wasn't like your own cousin could be your boyfriend — not outside of Shakespeare, anyway.

To tell you the truth, I didn't care much what

she thought any more. Pete was interested in me — there was no doubt about that now. I thought about our phone call again. He hadn't even minded me not saying anything. Usually, when I do that (it happens a fair bit — me being struck dumb) I get really embarrassed, and the other person just thinks I'm either a snob or a complete idiot. But he just seemed worried that I wasn't interested. *Me* not interested in *him*. It seemed a pretty weird thing to be worried about, but that was fine with me.

I couldn't wait till Saturday now, and of course it finally came around — though it seemed to take a hell of a long time. I made myself go for a long walk on the beach in the morning. It was getting cool these days, and there weren't too many people around. Cass and I walked all the way round to Red Bluff and back again, and it was nice just to walk along and look at the water and daydream. And imagine Pete was there, of course.

By the time I got home and had a shower and put on some clean clothes and a bit of make-up it was time for lunch. Dad and I cleared up afterwards, and he teased me a bit about Pete. I don't know who was more pleased — me or him! Well, I do know, of course, but Dad was pretty pleased as well. After that I just wandered round a bit, wondering what to do next. I really wanted to be caught in the middle of doing something cool this time, but I couldn't decide what. To tell you the truth, I wasn't really sure what Pete would think was cool — or if he thought about it at all. He seemed to me to be one of those people who just *were*, without ever thinking about it too much.

In the end, I was just standing in the middle of the lounge-room with a vacant expression on my face, when the doorbell rang. I jumped about ten feet in the air, and my heart started thumping. I wish I'd had time to check what I looked like or tidy my hair or something, but Mum and Dad were in the backyard, working on the vegie patch, so I just had to walk over and open the door.

Pete looked as beautiful as ever — and a lot cleaner than last time I saw him. He was obviously thinking pretty much the same thing.

'You sure look a lot better without dirt all over your face!' was the first thing he said to me. I just laughed.

'So do you!' I stood back a bit. 'Come in.'

We walked into the lounge-room and just stood there for a minute, smiling like a couple of idiots. Then he gave me a big hug.

'It's good to see you again.'

'You too,' I said, and gave him a kiss. 'Would you like some coffee?'

'Sure.'

So we went down to the kitchen, and I put the kettle on. We chatted a bit about what we'd been doing, then when the coffee was ready we opened the paper on the kitchen table and checked out what movies were on. Like Pete had said on the phone, it was so easy when we were together. It was like we'd known each other all our lives, only nicer — because there was still all sorts of things to find out about each other. But we laughed at the same things, and seemed to think the same things were worth being serious about. On the phone it was different. I couldn't see him — he wasn't smiling at me (or he might have been, but I couldn't see it). There was something about the way he smiled at me that made it easy to talk to him. It made me feel like everything was all right. But I'd get used to talking to him on the phone too, given half a chance. I was pretty sure of that.

So we sat there in the kitchen, nice and close together, drinking our coffee and looking at the paper. Sometimes he'd touch my hair or my hand, or just look at me. It's impossible to describe how good it made me feel. It was exciting — it gave me little butterflies in my stomach — but I felt comfortable too. And so happy I couldn't ever imagine feeling sad again. Nothing could get me down while I knew Pete was around.

We'd just decided we'd go to the nine o'clock session of *Father* (which was about this guy who murdered his family with a knife, and then went and married into another family — just so he could hack them up as well), when Mum came in from outside.

'Hello, Pete. You two decided on a film yet?'

'Yep,' he said, and told her about it. She shivered and laughed.

'You ghouls! I'd have nightmares for weeks!'

'Well, you don't have to come with us, Mrs Anderson,' Pete said, laughing at her. She just gave us both one of her looks.

She asked Pete if he wanted to stay for dinner then — which he did, of course — and then we caught the train into town. The film was good — some bits were pretty scary, some bits were just stupid (most horror films are like that) — and though Pete had his arm round me the whole way through he didn't, you know, try anything. I don't know exactly what he *could* try in a packed cinema, but you never know, do you? At least, I felt like there was so much I didn't know, I figured anything was possible.

Afterwards we went to this cafe in Bourke Street. We talked about the film a bit, and drank our cappucinos. It was nice, you know, but after a while I noticed Pete was looking at me — well, it's kind of hard to describe. It was sort of a warm look. It was nice, in one way, but it made me a bit uncomfortable, too. What was he thinking?

I was concentrating so hard on trying to read his mind, I kind of lost track of what he was saying. He reached over and took hold of my hand.

'Hello, hello... is there anybody in there?'

I did this silly laugh. I could feel my face heating up. He noticed, and leaned a bit closer.

'What's up?'

Have I mentioned how nice his voice is? I think I might have. It wasn't just how loud or soft it was, or how high or deep, though it was pretty perfect on those scales. It wasn't even the way he sounded like he was laughing, even with a straight face — though I liked that a lot too. What really made me go weak at the knees was that he sounded so kind whenever he talked to me. It's weird, isn't it? You'd think — or at least I did, before this — that you'd fall for a guy because he was tall, or good looking, or sexy, or cool, or something!

Well, Pete was all of those things — but what

really got me every time was that he was so kind. He was such a nice guy. He just looked and sounded like he cared. And that was what made me feel like I was floating.

So, when he leaned forward and squeezed my hand and looked at me — like that — I decided I might as well clear things up right now. God knows I'd said and done enough dumb things so far for him not to mind too much. I hoped.

'Well...' It was a pretty hard thing to talk about, all the same.

'Mmm?'

'It's just that...'

'What?'

'There's just one thing that's been worrying me...'

My face was lighting up the whole cafe by this time. He took hold of both my hands. 'What's been worrying you, little Kate?'

'Well, Lucy — you know Lucy McGregor — '

'I know Lucy.'

'— and Jamie Hamilton — '

'What about them?'

'The thing is...'

He put his forehead down on the table. 'Katie, *please*, get on with it.'

'They — ah — kind of warned me about you.'

Ooops! He looked a bit offended.

'What do you mean, warned you about me?'

'The thing is — it's just that — '

He just looked at me and raised his eyebrows. I leaned right over the table and whispered in his ear, 'I'm a virgin.'

He burst out laughing. My face went redder than even — if possible. Then he leaned over and took my face between his hands and kissed me. Right in the middle of the cafe.

'Kate Anderson, you are such a dag.'

'I know.'

'You thought I was going to rape you or something, did you?'

'No! No, it's just — I didn't know what you expected...'

He took hold of my hands again.

'I don't expect anything. Of course I'd like to — ah — '

It was his turn to look a bit embarrassed.

'Mmm,' I said.

'But I'm not going to force you to do anything. I just like to be with you. A lot. I like to look at you, and I like listening to you talk, and I like talking to you. You're different.'

'You can say that again.'

'But it's nice. That's what makes you special. That's why I've been making such a fool of myself over you.'

This was news to me!

'Have you?'

'My mates seem to think so. But then, they haven't met you. Lucy just told them about me visiting you last weekend.'

'Sorry — shouldn't I have said anything?'

'It doesn't worry me.'

I thought about it for a minute.

'But what's the problem? Don't you go to girls' houses or something?'

'If I do, I don't usually hang around much.'

'Mmm.'

'I told you you were special. And anyway, I had a good time.'

'I did too.'

'I liked your mum and dad, too. They're just as weird as you are.'

'Thanks very much! I hope I'm not as strange as them!'

He patted my hand. 'Not yet...'

'Watch it...'

We both laughed.

After that it was easy. We had another coffee, and just chatted. It's funny how easy it was to talk to him. It kept on surprising me. It wasn't like we talked about anything special, there just always seemed to be something to say, and everything seemed to lead to something else. And even on the train on the way home, when we didn't really say much to each other, it was just as good to sit there quietly and lean my head against his shoulder. In fact, it was perfect.

At my front gate we knew the night was finally over. It seemed a shame. Despite its ups and downs, it'd been pretty much a ten-out-of-ten night.

Pete put his arms around me. 'Katie?'

'Mmm?'

'If I kiss you, are you going to panic?'

I looked up at him. 'I'm more likely to panic if you don't kiss me!'

'Well then...'

As I said, pretty much a ten-out-of-ten night.

Chapter 9

I had no doubts now, and no worries. And it's incredible how happy I felt. You know, you go along most of the time — as long as nothing really terrible's happening — thinking you're happy. But you're not. You're just sort of not-sad. But now I was really, incredibly, stupendously, amazingly happy. Getting up in the morning was a pleasure. Going to school was fun. I enjoyed doing my homework and talking to my parents. Because all the time I knew Pete was there — that he really cared about me.

We saw a lot of each other these days. On the weekends we'd go out to the movies — I even got him along to see *All About Eve* — one of my favourite old films. He didn't seem to mind it too much. We drank about a million cappucinos in cafes all over town — we'd take a tram to some place we'd never been before, and suss out the best looking cafe. We went for walks on the beach with Cass and his dog, whose name was Dog. Catchy, eh? Sometimes he came round and had dinner with me and Mum and Dad, sometimes Pete and I just sat around — anywhere — and talked. Or even just sat. It didn't matter, as long as we were together. Which sounds kind of corny, I know. But there it is.

So I sang little songs to myself while I was getting dressed for school. I smiled all the time. I talked to old ladies in the street. And Mum and Dad were really pleased too. They liked Pete, and I think they were glad that at last I was having a good time — and doing all right at school into the bargain.

And that was another thing — school. It's amazing what a difference all this business made there too. Suddenly I was Somebody — and it wasn't that I'd changed. Or not that I could tell. But by now Lucy (who knew everything about everybody) was convinced that Pete Shardlow really was my boyfriend (or that I was his girlfriend, depending on how you looked at it), and she just couldn't be nice enough. She never actually apologised for laughing in my face — which was a shame. I'd had lots of daydreams about breaking the news to her — very casual, you know — just working some devastating piece of inside information into the conversation so she'd realise it was me who'd had the last laugh.

But she found out before I got the chance to tell her, and she just seemed to take it for granted. Her sources must be pretty good. Funny thing about Lucy. She knows everybody, and everyone knows her, and she's absolutely the coolest girl in school. But I get the feeling no one actually likes her that much. The price of power, I guess.

Anyway, now I was definitely In. With the people who counted, anyway. And I could be as smart as I liked in class, and no one was about to say anything — at least not to my face. The Good Time Girls all asked me to have lunch with them, offered me cigarettes, and what's more, didn't hassle me when I said no. Though I did eat my lunch with them sometimes — just for the fun of it. They'd sit around and talk about clothes and music and hairstyles (I picked up a lot of useful information), but the funniest was when they started talking about their boyfriends.

For a while I'd imagined that everyone with a boyfriend felt pretty much like I did, and that everyone's boyfriend was as perfect as mine. Wrong again. The conversations went something like this...

'How's Mark?'

'All right, I suppose. He really gave me the shits on Saturday night, though.'

'Why?'

'We were watching videos at his place, and he just lay there all night, ordering me around, telling me to make him coffee, or sandwiches, or turn the volume up or down. And making dumb jokes just in the best bits of the movies. Not that the movies were any good, because of course we couldn't get anything I wanted to see. And then he wouldn't even walk me home! He's such a jerk.'

And so on. Of course Mark Johnson played in the St Kilda under-19's. So he could be as much of a jerk as he wanted and Anna wasn't about to do anything about it. But I never really had much to say at times like that. They'd say to me, 'How's Pete?', and all I could say was 'Good!'. I couldn't think of a single bitchy thing to say about him.

Which was just fine with me.

I still spend most of my time at school with Jamie. I'd been a bit worried at first that he might be — well — jealous. But he wasn't. In fact, he was about as pleased as my dad, and every three or four days he'd check up and make sure things were still okay between Pete and me. I guess he didn't like to do it too often though, because

Jamie was the only one I could really talk to about Pete, so he usually ended up getting an earful. He'd say 'How's Pete?' and I'd be off, telling him really long boring stories about what Pete and me had done yesterday, and what he'd said to me on the phone the night before, and what he was wearing and how good it looked last time I saw him. Stuff like that. I just liked to be able to think about him out loud sometimes.

And Jamie was pretty good. He didn't mind too much. If it all got too boring, he'd just put his hand over my mouth or pretend to strangle me or something like that. I'd usually get the hint.

It was getting close to the middle of the year when Pete asked me to go to the football one Saturday with him and a few of his mates. I said yes, of course. I'd never been to a football game in Melbourne, but I knew what a big deal it was. And I even knew a little bit about the game — my dad grew up in Melbourne, and was always pretty keen on it.

I was nervous, though, too. I'd never met any of Pete's friends before, and I had a feeling they didn't really approve of me, or at least all the time he was spending with me. 'Making a fool of himself,' they'd said. And to tell you the truth, I hadn't forgotten what they'd looked like the day I saw them down the street with Pete either.

Like any minute they were going to throw a brick through a shop window or snatch an old lady's handbag or something like that.

But I tried not to let it worry me too much, and I felt like I had a pretty good grip on myself by the time Saturday came around. We were meeting them there — Pete and I caught the train into Richmond with the million other footy fans in their scarves and beanies. It's a nice feeling, in the crowd. Everyone talks to everyone else, argues about their favourite players and teams, all the little kids have guernseys on and kick little footies up and down the aisle. It was fun. It was a bit weird to hear how seriously grown people took what seemed to me to be just a pretty ordinary kind of game — but it was fun.

Anyway, we arrived and walked over to the gate where we were meeting Scott and Tim and the rest. There they were. I think I was secretly hoping that when we arrived they'd be completely different to the guys I'd seen — nice respectable guys with normal haircuts and proper shoes. Nope. They were the same old bunch of thugs. I started to feel a bit sick. When we got there they all sort of went 'aaarrrgh' and slapped each other on the back and stuff like that. Then Pete introduced me and they all said 'Hi', normal enough, I guess.

There was one other girl there — Cindy. Can you believe it? Cindy. She was tall, and pretty thin too. I think she looked extra-skinny because her jeans were so tight. She was wearing white ankle-boots and smoking a menthol cigarette, and when she talked her voice was really high-pitched. Maybe that was because of the jeans, too. I was pretty interested to see her sit down when we got inside, but she seemed to manage it okay.

So that was the crowd I was with. Actually, it wasn't too bad during the game. The guys talked to each other, and Cindy just went 'Hee-hee-hee-hee-hee' whenever one of them make a joke. And I just smiled a lot. And watched the game. Watching the game was good, really. I still couldn't see why people got so carried away, but it was exciting. And some of the players were really gorgeous. Great legs. I got through the half-time break by smiling more than ever, and when the final siren went I felt like I could relax. I'd got through it pretty well, I thought.

Then as we were walking out the gates again (along with about two million other people), Pete said, 'Well, where to now?'

'How about the Corner?'

'Sure,' Pete said.

I wasn't quite sure what this meant — except

that I wasn't going home yet. I actually thought for a minute we were all going to go and stand on a corner somewhere (and maybe wait for some old lady to take her eyes off her handbag) — but it turned out to be something pretty much as bad. Now I might be a semi-dag, but I'm not a complete suck. At some other time I might've enjoyed going to a pub, if it was somewhere nice, with good people — and especially if we could've waited six months till I was legal. But the Corner Hotel was the filthiest, grottiest, dingiest hole I'd ever seen in my life. Not that I'm a pub expert. But it was hard to imagine anything worse.

We sat at a table that was decorated with nice patterns of cigarette ash glued to spilt beer, and Tim (or was it Scott or George?) took orders for drinks. Everyone else ordered pots — and then it was my turn. I didn't want to drink beer. I didn't know what to say. I had this kind of picture of me taking my first sip and some bouncer grabbing me by the collar and demanding ID — then turfing me out the door. Did they do that? I didn't know, but I wasn't too keen on taking the chance. So I just squeaked, 'I'll have a Coke.'

The other guys were looking at me pretty strangely, but Pete just smiled and squeezed my hand under the table.

It didn't get my evening off to a great start.

The guys sat there talking and joking away, and Cindy leaned back in her chair smoking her menthol cigarettes (with a gold band on the filter), and I sat sort of hunched up sipping my Coke and wishing I was somewhere else. I watched Pete, too. Well, let's face it, I always liked watching Pete, but tonight was especially interesting. I felt like I knew him so well — it was weird watching him be 'one of the boys'.

It wasn't that he was so different. They talked about different things to what Pete and I talked about — that was fair enough, I guess. What surprised me (I don't know why), was that he was just as relaxed and funny and normal as when he was talking to me or Mum and Dad. Only different. One of the boys. It was something I'd never got the hang of — being able to get along with all kinds of people. That's what made Pete so cool — and Lucy too, in her own way. Just being able to be yourself, and kind of *make* people like you all the same.

I felt worse and worse as the night went on. I really wanted to go home, I really wanted to get out of the pub, I wanted to be able to join in the conversation or make a joke they'd all laugh at — just something so I didn't feel quite so much like I was from another planet. None of these things happened though. I just had to sit there, sipping my Coke (I didn't even like Coke!), smiling till my face ached. I felt like it'd never end.

It did though, eventually. I had a quiet panic when one of the guys (was it Tim or Dave or George or Scott?) suggested we go somewhere else for more beer and pizza — but Pete must've seen the look on my face, and said he'd take me home. I smiled a real smile for the first time all day, and said goodbye to everyone.

It was so good to be back on the train — just me and Pete. The football crowds were all home by now, watching the replay on TV. The carriage was nearly empty, and I lay back with my feet on the seat opposite and my head on his shoulder, just relaxing. It was the first time I'd felt really relaxed all day. Every now and then Pete kissed the top of my head, and sometimes I'd turn my face up so I could kiss him back. I felt safe again.

Chapter 10

I thought a lot about that afternoon at the football. It wasn't just that I'd had a pretty rotten time — though that was part of it. What really got to me, what I really wished, was that I could get a grip on myself. I really wished I could learn the secret of being cool. Not necessarily like Lucy — she was fun, but I don't think she was a very nice person. I don't think *anyone* thought she was a very nice person, but then again I don't think anyone cared that much.

I just wanted to feel all right. I wanted to be able to talk to people I didn't know, and not make a fool of myself — or make them feel uncomfortable. It wasn't even that I wanted to be great mates with everyone. But people like Suzy, the girl I'd met at Lucy's party — I would've liked to have got to know her better. Instead I just ended up making her think I was a weirdo. But what did you say to strangers? Did you talk about the weather? I'd never heard Pete talking about the weather. He just seemed to *know*. Maybe that's all there was to it, after all. Maybe some people just had it, and some didn't.

Maybe I was doomed to be a semi-dag for the rest of my life.

I tried talking to Jamie about it, but he wasn't much help. He just told me not to be stupid, basically. He said there was nothing wrong with me, not to worry about what other people thought — that some people were shy, and some not so shy. It didn't make me feel a whole lot better.

On Wednesday Pete came round and we went out for a walk on the beach, along with Cass and Dog.

The beach was almost deserted these days, except for a couple of other people with their dogs, and one maniac swimmer. It was nice just to walk along kicking up sand and listening to the water swish. The surf wasn't great at Sandringham, but it was peaceful.

'Did you have a good time on Saturday?' Pete asked.

'Mmm,' I said.

'Does that mean mmm-yes or mmm-sort of?'

I smiled. 'Mmm-sort of.'

'Why?'

'I felt... I didn't really feel part of it, you know? And I felt like your mates didn't like me all that much.'

'They thought you were pretty cute, actually. They were just a bit — shy, I guess.'

I was surprised. That hadn't exactly been my impression. I mean, they didn't look like the shy types to me. I said so.

'Well, I guess you don't really know them, do you,' Pete said. 'They're different to you. Different families, they grew up differently. It doesn't mean they're any better or worse — most of them grew up pretty much like me.'

Pete had told me a bit about his life, and I'd met his mum. She was big and blonde (like Pete) and laughed a lot and was secretary of the local football club. His dad had run off to New Zealand with some other woman when Pete was still in primary school. Since then it'd just been him and his mum and his big brother Matthew. Though Matthew had left home and got married a couple of years ago, so I'd never seen him.

They'd never had much money. They used to live in a housing commission flat until his mum had got a job. Now she worked a day shift in one of the local pubs. And Pete had been in a bit of trouble when he was younger, thought I think he behaved himself pretty well these days. But that's why his friends were what they were. And I guess in his heart Pete was still a bit of a thug himself — and probably always would be. But that was part of why I liked him so much.

The thing was, though, that he *wasn't* like those other guys. He might say it was just that I didn't know them, but it was more than that. He might tease me about the way I talked (he reckoned I was the only girl in Melbourne who said 'however'), and joke about being from the wrong side of the tracks, but in heaps of ways he was really a lot like me. I said, 'But you're different. You weren't shy when you met me. Or my parents. And you're not a — not a total lout, whatever you might say.'

He laughed. 'So?'

I shrugged. As usual, I found it kind of hard to get to the point. We walked along a bit further, then I had to ask, 'But why?'

He gave me a bit of a squeeze. 'I don't know, Katie. Does it matter?'

'It doesn't matter... it's just that...'

'Oh no!'

'What?'

'You're not going to start another "Oh well, the

thing is, it's just that..." are you? We'll be here till midnight!'

I just looked at him.

'I was just going to say that I wanted to know because...'

'Mmm?'

'You *are* different from those other guys — your friends. You can be mates with them, and still talk to me, and my parents, your mum, or Lucy, or anyone. You always seem to know the right thing to say. You're always relaxed about — people.'

'I still don't see what you're getting at.'

'If you can be, why can't I?'

It sounded a bit dumb, but Pete was used to that. He took hold of my hand and we walked back up the beach a bit to where high tide had made a kind of bench, and we sat down.

'It worries you, does it?'

'Yeah. It didn't — or maybe I just didn't notice, I never really met anyone new, much. But now everything's different. There are people — everywhere! I just don't know what to say to them... and I'd like to.'

'You don't have to talk to every single one of them, you know.'

'You know what I mean. I'm serious.'

He thought about it a minute, and then started talking, slowly.

'It's kind of hard to explain… I never really thought about it much. There are just — well, I was never really all that shy. I always just liked meeting people, you know? Finding out about them — what they think, how they live, what they do. You can go along thinking everyone's pretty much like everyone else — but they're not. Even people you think look really ordinary and boring sometimes have the most amazing lives.'

Sure, but it didn't really answer my question. He tried again.

'But you're interested in people too — you know you are. You're a real sticky-beak some of the time. It's not as if you don't want to know.'

'So?'

He was quiet for a bit. I could almost hear the cogs turning over. He may not be able to help me to Coolness, but I sure appreciated the effort he was making. Then he said, 'What do you think about when you meet new people?'

'What do you mean?'

'Well, say I introduced you to — I don't know, anyone — Dave. What'd be going through your mind?'

'I'd be thinking — help!'

'Why?'

'Afraid I'd say the wrong thing, make a fool of myself, I guess. God knows it's happened often enough.'

'Well, that's the first thing, isn't it? You have to stop worrying. What's it matter what people think of you? I know you're all right, you know you're all right. What's there to worry about?'

'But why can't I act like I'm all right. That's the thing. I might be like a perfectly normal person talking to you now... but my mind just goes completely blank. I freeze. I don't know what to say to them.'

'But what are you thinking?'

'I told you — nothing!'

'There must be something going on in your head.'

I thought about it. 'I guess if I'm thinking anything, I'm wondering what the hell I'm going to say to them, and how dumb I must look standing there like a dodo.'

'Well, that's it then.'

'What then?'

'Stop thinking about yourself. Think about the other person — the one you're meeting. You only have to look at someone, and you start wondering things about them, don't you? Well, if you really can't think of anything to say, ask them something about themselves.' He couldn't help adding, 'Something polite. But most of the time, other people help you out too. You just have to listen to what they're saying. It's the same thing. If you stop thinking about what you're thinking, and pay attention to what they're saying, you'll be fine.'

'As easy as that?'

'Trust me.'

I looked up at him. He was smiling, sort of teasing me, but sort of serious too. And I did trust him. It was worth a try at least. It actually made pretty good sense. I gave him a big hug and said, 'You're wonderful.'

He didn't seem to mind that too much.

It was starting to get dark by this time, so we wandered back up to the house. Mum was talking on the phone when we walked in, and she looked up and said, 'Kate, it's for you.'

I took the phone. It was Lucy. It was Party Time again. We had our mid-year exams coming up, and she was organising something for after that — did I want to come along. And Pete, of course. I held the receiver against my chest.

'Do you want t go to Lucy's party, Friday after exams?'

'Sure.'

Mum was sitting at the dining table, marking geography assisgnments — she was teaching at the local primary school.

'Mum, is it all right if Pete and I got to Lucy's

party…'

'…the Friday after exams? That's fine with me, Katie.'

So I said to Lucy, 'Sure,' and we arranged the time and stuff. When I hung up I flopped down on the chair next to Pete, and he kind of rolled his eyes.

'That's something to look forward to.'

'Don't you want to go?'

'Sure,' he said.

'What's up then.'

'Just Lucy.'

I raised my eyebrows. I'd always thought she and Pete were fairly close — I know they'd spent a bit of time together when they were younger.

'Don't get me wrong,' he said when he saw my face. 'It's not that I don't like her, most of the time. Well, as much as you can like anyone who doesn't like anyone but herself — it's just that she's a bit of a Jekyll and Hyde.'

I hadn't forgotten what she'd been like at her last party.

'Mmm,' I said.

Later, as we were saying goodbye — which seemed to take longer and longer every day — I said, 'Well, I'm looking forward to the party, anyway.'

'Why?'

'So I can practise my new People Skills, of course!'

Pete just laughed.

Chapter 11

I didn't see much of Pete for a while. We were both working pretty hard for the exams. You try and tell yourself it doesn't matter that much — it's not like The Big One — but you can't help getting a bit uptight about everything. So I was doubly — triply — glad when the night of the party came. One — I'd see Pete again (this was a pretty big Number One). Two — it was all over — at least for a few months. And three — although Pete had laughed at me — I *was* looking forward to trying out some of the things he'd said to me. I just hoped there'd be some people there I didn't know.

I was pretty confident about dressing myself these days — no need for Jamie's help in that department this time. In fact, I was actually looking forward to this party. I had clothes to wear, there'd be a whole lot of people I knew, I knew the rules, what to expect — and, of course, I had Pete. It was amazing what a difference he'd made in my life. Jamie was good — he was still a great friend. But it wasn't the same. There were some things he just couldn't help me with. Like parents. No matter how understanding they are, or how much they love you, sometimes they're just no help at all.

But now I had Pete. And whenever — if ever — I felt sad, or angry, or lonely, all I had to do was remember he was there, and I felt better. And when I felt good, he was always ready to laugh, and feel good with me. Actually, that's one of the things I liked best about Pete. He might make fun of me, but he always understood my jokes. Which is more important than you'd think.

So off I went on Friday night, pretty full of beans. I was still a bit nervous, but it was a nice kind of nervousness this time. To put it another way, I didn't feel like I was going to puke — just kind of excited.

When we actually walked into Lucy's house, I balked a bit. It was just as dark and noisy and smelly as I remembered, and I wondered again why people made such a big deal about parties. Still, I was going to enjoy this one, or die trying.

Well, in the end I did enjoy myself. At first I saw a few people I knew, mainly from school, and had a talk to them. That was my warm-up. Then I saw the girl I'd met last time — Jamie's neighbour Suzy. I said hi, and she seemed to remember me, and asked how I thought I went in exams. Which wasn't scary at all really. I remembered Jamie had said she was in first year uni, doing literature and sociology, so I asked her a couple of things about that. And pretty soon we were going on like old friends, talking about books and things and what we wanted to do When We Grew Up. It was easy, really, and interesting too.

A bit later she went off to talk to some other friends of hers, so I headed back to Pete. He was standing near the back door, talking to some friends, so I went over and said hello. It was a couple of the guys we'd been to the footy with (was it Dave or Scott or Grant or George?).

Luckily Pete said, 'Kate, you remember Scott and Dave, don't you?'

So I smiled and said yes. Now I just had to work out which was which! We stood around for a bit, then Pete went off to the kitchen to get a drink, and I was left with Scott and Dave. Dave and Scott. We smiled at each other a bit, then I decided to take the plunge.

I started off by asking him (Dave? Scott?) how

he got to know Pete — and before long we were talking about things we used to do when we were kids, and I told him a bit about the way things were in South Australia, and he told me about how his grandfather used to work at a mine outside Bendigo. I even discovered which one was Dave and which Scott. Pretty successful all round.

When Pete came back I think he was a bit surprised to see us all chatting away — but he knew what was going on too. He put his arm round me and whispered, 'Practising?'

I smiled up at him. 'You bet.'

And he gave me another squeeze. He and the guys started talking about something they'd been on before I arrived — football, I think. I didn't try to join in. I was happy enough to stand there smiling, with Pete's arm round me. Only this time I was smiling because I really was happy. I felt like I didn't need to talk all the time. Because I knew if I wanted to, I could.

On the way home in a taxi, I leaned right back and snuggled up against Pete. I felt pretty good about myself. He knew it too.

'Proud of yourself?'

'Uh-huh.'

'Told you it was easy, didn't I?'

'Right again. Ten out of ten.'

'Have I changed your life for ever?'

I looked up at him for a minute. He was joking, but it wasn't as silly as it sounded. Not just about me being able to go to parties and actually talk to people. All kinds of things. Pete really had made a big difference to me — and I'd never go back to the way I was again. So I just said, 'Yes.'

He looked at me, serious too. Then he touched my face, really gently, then kissed me.

It was the beginning of a beautiful weekend. Not that we did anything much out of the ordinary. We walked on the beach, we went to the movies, we lolled round the house watching TV and annoying Mum in her vege patch. But it was wonderful. I'd thought things couldn't possibly get any better — but they had. I felt like I just couldn't be any happier, and though we didn't talk about it, Pete looked like he felt pretty much the same way.

But when I next saw Pete he wasn't looking so happy. Results had come out on Wednesday, and that night he came round to see me. We were going to do a bit of study (it seemed like it'd never end!) — but he wanted to go for a walk first. It was pretty obvious something was on his mind. We walked up Bridge Street and did a lap of the park, then headed down to the beach. He didn't say anything, just held onto my hand and frowned.

Eventually I couldn't bear it any more, and asked him what was up.

'I'm thinking about dropping out.'

'What?'

'I'm leaving school. There's no point hanging round any more. It's a waste of time.'

'Don't be stupid,' I said.

Well, it was a pretty dumb thing to say. But it made him angry and he dropped my hand.

'You don't know what it's like.'

'Of course I know what school's like.'

'That's not what I meant. It's different for you.'

'Why?'

He walked along kicking up sand, frowning more than ever. I just let him go for a while, then dragged him up the beach to a seat on the bluff.

'Well, come on. Talk to me.'

'There's nothing to talk about.'

'I see. So you're leaving school for no reason at all?'

'I didn't say that!'

'Then what is it?'

He just sat there.

'Look, if you can't tell me, who can you tell?'

He looked at me for a minute. 'I failed,' he said.

'What?'

'Everything.'

'You failed everything?'

It was sort of hard to imagine someone failing *everything*.

'Thanks for your support.' And he got up from the bench and started to walk away.

'Peter Shardlow — get back here this minute. How am I supposed to help you if you growl and scratch me every time I open my mouth?'

He stood for a minute on the bluff, then came and sat down again. But he still wasn't smiling.

Eventually I said, 'Look, I didn't mean to be rude — it's just that I don't understand why. You're not stupid.'

'Aren't I?'

'Of course not. Except for just now, sulking and scowling like a two year old. What went wrong?'

'I don't know! The thing is, nothing's ever gone right. I must be just a blockhead.'

'Well you're not. You know that and so do I.'

'Well, what other reason is there? I've never been much good with schoolwork — I've usually managed to bluff my way though, you know. But this is different. For one thing, the whole point of bluffing your way through was to get onto the next year. Then the next year you'd do the same thing. Only now it's different. You can't bluff. And even if you did, what's the point? There's no next year — unless you want to go to uni. And even if I did want to go, I'd never get through.

The whole thing's just hopeless.'

'It's not hopeless. It can't be, because you're not that dumb. If you could do anything you wanted — what would you do?'

He shrugged. 'I don't know. That's part of the problem. I just don't know what I want — so what's the point?'

I wished he'd stop saying that.

'I can't believe you couldn't pass if you tried.'

'But I do try. Sort of. I just never get anywhere. I mean, I try for a while, but it doesn't make any difference — so I just give up.'

'Mmm.'

I sat there for a while. It was hard to know what to do. And he was being so prickly. It didn't help.

After a while I said, 'Well, there are some things I could try to help you with. Maybe if you talked about the things you didn't understand, I could help you out. Especially with English.'

I was worried that he'd be offended, but he didn't seem to be.

'Could you help, do you think?'

'I could try.'

'Well, that's all right for English. But even if you can help, what about my science or maths subjects? You don't know anything about it.'

He was right. Maths and science weren't exactly my strong points. Then I had an idea.

I mentally crossed my fingers and said, 'Dad knows about that stuff though — he's an engineer. At least, I'm not sure about biol, but maths and chemistry is right up his alley. Maybe he could help you out.'

'Do you think he would though? I mean, why should he?'

'Because I'd ask him to. Or you could. He likes you a lot, you know.'

Pete looked surprised. I don't know why, because it always seemed pretty obvious to me that Dad liked Pete, and not just because he was a friend of mine. But maybe Pete never really thought about people's parents liking him or not. Parents were a bit like that. Just sort of *there*.

'I don't know,' he said.

'Look, there's no harm in asking, is there? And even if he can't, I can still help you with English. And maybe we could find someone else to help you with the other stuff. It's worth trying, isn't it? And at least it's better than doing nothing — dropping out.'

We were both pretty convinced by my arguments — and Pete looked like he was feeling much better as we headed off home.

He was staying for dinner that night, so when Mum had gone off into the lounge-room with her coffee and Dad was stacking the dishwasher, I pushed Pete into the kitchen and left him to it. We'd decided it was probably better if Pete asked himself. He said he'd feel like a baby doing it any other way. So I went off to sit with Mum, and tell her all about it. I'd actually promised Pete not to tell anyone, but I figured I could trust Mum with something like that. And maybe she'd have some helpful advice. She was pretty keen on giving out helpful advice, as a rule.

Mum didn't have much to say in the end, except she thought I'd done the right thing. And of course Dad said yes. And the good thing was, not only did he not mind, he was actually glad to help out. I think he was always a bit disappointed I wasn't more interested in that kind of stuff. He was glad I liked Shakespeare, of course — but maybe he thought it would've been even better if I'd liked science as well.

Anyway, now he had someone to talk about sine curves, and molecular structure with — and Pete had someone to help him out. And if he didn't look exactly happy, he looked much better.

I didn't walk with him up to the corner any more — it was too dark and cold these nights. But I always went outside the gate with him — my compromise.

'I don't know if it'll do any good, Katie — but thanks for your help,' he said.

I gave him a hug.

'Of course it'll help. You know you can do absolutely anything you put your mind to.' Mum hadn't said I should tell him that, but if she'd remembered she would have.

Pete held me really tightly. It was a bit hard to breathe, but nice. We just stood there for a while like that, then he let go and took my face between both his hands. He looked serious, and I was a bit afraid of what he was going to say or do. But he just kissed me, and looked at me again, and said, 'I love you, Katie.'

That wasn't so bad, was it?

Chapter 12

You think I didn't wear that like a halo for the rest of the week!

'I love you'! How about that! I floated. I danced. I couldn't stop smiling. It amazed me how I just kept getting happier and happier. Just when I thought I was as happy as I could possibly get — things got better! I felt... electrified. Just buzzing with life. Mum noticed I was acting a bit strangely, and asked me what was the matter. I was feeling so fantastic, I just said, 'He loves me!' and she said, 'I knew that weeks ago.'

But even that kind of stupid remark couldn't bring me down.

I rang Pete up first thing the next morning, and told him since there was only a few months to go till exams, he'd better get over here and start studying. He didn't seem to see anything wrong with that. He said, in his most serious voice — which is exactly when he's least serious — 'Very sensible, Kate. I'll be there in ten minutes.'

And he was.

Naturally, we couldn't get down to work right away. You have to warm up to these things. So we went down to the beach, and as soon as we were out of sight of the dog walkers we flopped down in the sand and put our arms round each other. We just lay there for a little while, and then we kissed for a little while. Well, all right, quite a long while.

I said, 'Pete, there's something important I've been meaning to tell you… I should've told you last night, but, well… it just went completely out of my head.'

He sat on his elbows, looking pretty worried. Looking pretty gorgeous, too.

'I love you,' I said.

And he just laughed and squeezed me tighter than ever. I see what they mean when they say 'love hurts'. I felt like my ribs were breaking. But he could've crushed me to death just then, and I would have died happy.

Well, by the time we finally made it back to the house, it was fair to say we were warmed up. In fact we were so warmed up it was harder than ever to get down to work. But finally Dad said, 'Are you two going to do some work, or just moon around the house all day?'

He was smiling, but that did the trick. We got out our books, made some coffee, and settled down at the dining-table.

'Well,' he said, 'where should we start?'

'Shakespeare,' I said, seeing it was my specialty.

He put his head down on the table. 'I don't know if this is going to work, Kate. You just have to mention the word Shakespeare and I go blank. I get bored just saying *Hamlet*. I mean, who ever heard of anyone called Hamlet? How can you take it seriously?'

'Mr Shardlow.' I decided I hard to be firm. 'Stop panicking, and pay attention. You're as bad as me! Worse — because at least books can't think you're an idiot, or talk about you behind your back, or ignore you at parties. They're totally harmless — that's the first thing to remember.'

'They're totally harmless,' he said. He didn't sound too convinced, but I didn't let it put me off.

'The first thing is to have a bit of confidence in yourself. I know you're all right, you know you're all right — so what is there to worry about? Someone I'm very close to told me that. It's pretty good advice.'

He smiled at that at least.

'So, stop thinking you're a blockhead — which you're not — and just remember you're bigger than it. It's only a book.'

'It's only a book.'

'Good. Now, the next thing — the most important thing — is to be a bit interested. Stop thinking about yourself, and start thinking about the book.'

'Katie, will you stop taking the piss and tell me what the bloody thing's about?'

'I'm serious.'

'But it's completely different — people *are* interesting. It's natural to want to know about them. Books are just — books.'

'Wrong. Books are about people — interesting people. You just have to get to know them a bit. Look...'

And I opened up good old *Hamlet*, and we started to go through it from Act I, with me sort of translating as we went. Eventually he seemed to be getting the hang of it.

'He sounds like a psychopath.'

'Exactly. He's losing his mind.'

'Because his mother's married his father's brother as soon as his father was dead — and he thinks his father's brother murdered his father just to get into bed with his mother.'

'And be King of Denmark. Wouldn't you be starting to feel a bit unhinged?'

'Mmm.'

' "Oh that this too, too solid flesh would melt" — like how I feel when I'm kissing you, and I wish we could just dissolve together?'

'Not exactly. More like when you've just found out you've failed every single subject, and wish you could just vanish into thin air... But thanks for the thought.'

'Mmm.'

And so on. In the end he got quite into the story — and though he never stopped moaning about the way they talked, at least he understood what was going on. I guess he'd never get much pleasure from Shakespeare — but he sure had a better chance of passing.

We broke for dinner, and after that Dad took over. I sat in the lounge-room re-reading *Pride and Prejudice* while Mum watched TV; and Dad and Pete sat at the dining-table, scribbling graphs and equations and talking gibberish. I don't know how Pete could complain about the way *Hamlet* talked. At least he never said things like 'alpha gamma sine hypotenuse' — or whatever it was they were going on about. I wondered if the science coaching would really be much help. It beats me how anyone can even understand the questions, let alone answer them.

But when the party broke up, and I was sitting on the fence talking to Pete, he semed pretty cheerful about it all. Apparently he'd discovered how to work out just how smashed up you'd be if a car going at twenty kilometres an hour ran into you while you were walking at two kilometres an hour. Good stuff, eh? It didn't seem quite as interesting to me as the discussion of morality, justice and racism in *The Merchant of Venice*, but there you go. It takes all kinds to make up the world, doesn't it?

And as I said, I was walking on air all week. If I'd felt good last week because I'd finally worked out how not to be a complete dork in public places (with a little help from my friend), I felt doubly good now that I was helping Pete find out how not to be a complete dork in the exam room. And he loved me. Let's not forget that. He loved me — and nothing else really mattered.

We saw even more of each other these days. When he wasn't round at my place exchanging sine curves with my dad, we were lying on his bedroom floor, arguing about why it was inevitable that Gertrude should drink the poison before Hamlet. And then, of course, sometimes we'd just lie on his bedroom floor, and not think about study at all.

I was starting to think seriously about that S word again. I'd put it out of my mind after our talk in the cafe that night, and Pete had never mentioned it again. But now, now and then, pretty often, I'd been thinking it really might be kind of nice. I felt like I wanted to do it — I just didn't really want to talk about it. That is, I wouldn't have minded talking about it if he'd brought the subject up. But he didn't, and I wasn't game enough to do it all by myself. Introduce the subject, I mean.

So we just left things as they were. In some ways I wished I hadn't made such a big deal of it when we'd first talked about it. I think it'd made him not want to bring it up again. But on the other hand, in lots of ways I was happy to leave things as they were. I loved holding him and kissing him, I loved being with him and talking to him, I loved just looking at him. I loved him. I felt like that was enough for the moment. Anything more — especially with our end of year exams looming up — would have been a big complication I just didn't need.

But we were close — closer than we'd ever been. On the nights we didn't see each other, we always called each other up — just to talk about what we'd done that day, and when we'd see each other next, and (like the Stevie Wonder song I'd always thought was so corny) just to say 'I love you'. It was nice to be able to say it, and to hear the other person say it back. And to mean it.

It was amazing how quickly time went in those days. I think it was partly because there was always something to look forward to the next day. So you'd race through Monday, just to get to Tuesday. And on Tuesday you couldn't wait for Wednesday, because there was a fair chance that was going to be even better. I'd settled down a bit. I didn't feel so insanely happy so much, but I still felt good — all the time — and I loved Pete as much — more — than ever. So I kind of gutsed down time. I felt like I had to eat up all this happiness while I could, and before I knew it we were in September, and I could count on my fingers the weeks until exam-time.

One night we were sitting on the fence, just talking, after Dad and Pete had been studying. Well, Dad hadn't been doing much study, but you get what I mean. I was feeling pretty hopeful about Pete's chances at the end of the year. He was never going to write a great novel, but he had all the basic ideas. And Dad reckoned he was actually really good at science and maths, once they'd got a few basic things sorted out. But Pete still wasn't too sure. He'd got so used to thinking he wasn't any good at school, I guess it was kind of hard for him to realise that he was. So I told him what Dad had said, to cheer him up.

He said, 'Oh, I haven't got too many problems with that stuff any more, but well, English — I don't know if you're ever going to be able to do anything with me.'

I was about to tell him how great he was going there, too, but he went on, 'But did you know...'

He was off. Some amazing mathematical fact he'd discovered that night. The problem with Pete's amazing mathematical facts was, the more he learned, the longer his True Science Stories got, and the less I understood them. And tonight's was a doozy. I must've sat there for twenty minutes, freezing to death, while he went on about velocity mass equilibrium hyperbolic beta median theta — or something like that. And at the end he said, 'Incredible, isn't it?'

I had to agree it was pretty incredible. What else could I say? And then at last he put his arms round me and kissed me and told me how wonderful I was. And I felt like he could've told me the story all over again, and I wouldn't have minded.

Not too much, anyway.

Chapter 13

It was only a few weeks till exams when Pete asked me if I wanted to go to the footy again. One of the finals. So I said sure, and I think Dad was a bit jealous. He really liked football, but since Mum had started working full-time again, they didn't see a lot of each other. And she wasn't all that keen on footy. So on Saturdays he stayed home with her and helped with the shopping, and then later on watched replays in secret on video while she was marking assignments. I don't think he minded too much normally, but I know he would've liked to go to that game.

In the end, he probably would've had a better time than me. And Pete might have, too. We went in on the train again, which was just as much fun as last time. Better, really, because everyone was really excited, and even the little kids had stopped kicking their plastic footies in the aisle and were arguing about which player was better than which, and why their favourite football team would wipe the ground with the opposition. It's always funny to hear little kids talking just like their parents. Not to mention the parents talking just like their kids.

Anyway, we and the million other people poured off the train at Richmond, then stood like we were set in concrete, trying to get in the gates. It drove me crazy, just standing there for almost an hour. No one else seemed to mind too much. It was all part of the business of going to a final, I guess. But I wasn't enough of a fan to make it worth while. And then, once we were finally inside, we had to look for Dave and Grant and Scott. Of course, they hadn't had the sense to stick together, so once we'd found Dave, then we had to go on a hunt for Grant, who told us he'd left Scott waiting somewhere else on the other side of the ground — so we had to go and find him too.

By the time everyone found everyone else, I was just about ready to go home again, but the fun had only just started. Next was the half-day trek to find our seats, which turned out to be not seats at all, but just a big place half the population of Melbourne was standing. I couldn't believe we were going to stand up for the whole game, and for a minute I thought about pretending to faint — you know, 'swoon', like the ladies in books who wore their corsets too tight. But even if I did pretend to faint, I wasn't completely sure anyone would notice, because by then the game had started.

I honestly don't know how I did it. As I said, I'm not very tall, so I couldn't see a thing, even if I'd wanted to. My legs were aching and my feet were aching and my head was aching — by half-time I was really ready to murder someone. At least around that time everyone poured out of the stand to get beer and pies, so I could put my coat on the ground and sit on that for a while, stretching my ankles and wriggling my toes. Then the siren sounded, and it was on again.

I really did feel a bit sick by the time the game was over and we'd struggled out the gates again. It was almost dark too. And then — of course — all the guys wanted to go to the pub again. So off we went.

I guess I could've gone home by myself. But I hated to leave Pete. I knew he wanted me to stay, and I know if I'd gone home, I would have missed him too, and regretted it. So I stayed on, in the pub which was just as filthy and dingy as I remembered, only more crowded. Everyone was talking football at the tops of their voices, the TV over the bar was showing the replay, everywhere you looked there were fat guys in guernseys and duffle coats, and I decided then and there I was never, ever going to a football game again as long as I lived.

I didn't even try to make conversation this time; I didn't even bother to smile unless someone looked right at me. Most of the time I just leaned back in my chair with my eyes half closed, wishing it was all over. It was even worse than last time, because at least then I'd been trying to make a good impression, even if it wasn't all that successful. Tonight I really wished everyone in the pub would just drop dead. In fact, about the only time I enjoyed myself all night was when I was imagining, with my eyes half shut, that every single person there suddenly went quiet and fell down, in some kind of mass football-fit, and I just got up and walked out over the bodies and went home.

But it didn't happen. I just had to sit there, getting more and more tired and more and more annoyed every minute. And to make it worse, Pete hardly looked at me all night. He was too busy talking about — you guessed it — football.

At last the party broke up, and, like last time, we went home when the rest of the guys went out for pizza. I knew Pete would've really liked to go this time, but I just couldn't do it. He said to me, kind of hopefully, 'What would you like to do, Katie?'

And I said, 'Go home.'

So we did.

I had a little snooze on the train, which was nice. It was warm and dry and it was so good to have Pete's arm round me again and his head resting on mine. And it was quiet, too, compared with the pub. So I slept all the way to Sandringham, and felt much better when I woke up again. We walked really slowly back to the house with our arms round each other, not saying much, and I asked Pete in for a coffee and something to eat when we got there.

It was unbelievably good to sit in front of the fire in a comfortable chair, and with good food in my stomach and a cup of coffee in my hand. And to have my boyfriend's undivided attention. Mum and Dad were out to dinner, so we had the whole place to ourselves, at least for a couple of hours. Which was plenty of time to make up for the rest of the day, really. We sure made good use of it, anyway.

When Mum and Dad came home, I walked with Pete out to the gate. He didn't hang around too long — it was late, and we were both pretty tired. But he did put his arms round me, and kiss me, and tell me how much he loved me. Which really made the rest of the day worthwhile.

On Sunday morning Jamie phoned. It was good to hear his voice — though we still saw a lot of each other at school, he didn't call me (or me him) much these days. I was kept pretty busy with a combination of Pete and study, and I guess he knew that.

So we talked for a while about our weekend. I told him about my Saturday, which he seemed to think was pretty funny. And his team had won the basketball finals, so he was in a really good mood, and it made me feel better about my day at the footy to hear him laugh about it. That was the really good thing about Jamie. Nothing ever worried him too much, and he always made you feel that the things that were worrying you didn't matter too much either.

After we'd caught up on all the gossip he said, 'Are you doing anything next Saturday night?'

'Why?' I always spent my Saturday nights with Pete — it was a kind of rule. But we hadn't actually planned anything, so I waited to hear what Jamie had to say for himself.

'Do you remember Suzy, my next door neighbour?'

'Yeah — I had a talk with her at Lucy's last party.'

'Well, she's having some people round to her place for dinner next weekend. She's asked me, and I thought you might like to come along, seeing as everyone else will be bookworms like you. I thought you could be my translator.' Jamie wasn't much of a reader.

I thought about it for a minute. It sounded great. Since I'd learned how to actually have conversations, I liked to meet people. Not all of them turned out to be the type of person you wanted to get to know, but I liked the idea of finding some people who didn't think I was mentally unstable just because I liked Shakespeare.

But there was Pete. I knew he'd be expecting to see me over the weekend. And I knew he wouldn't be too pleased if I suddenly said, 'Oh, by the way, I can't see you on Saturday, I'm going to a dinner party.'

So I asked, 'Would Pete be able to come, do you think?'

'I guess so. I can ask Suzy for you if you like.'

So I asked him to do that, and pretty soon after that we hung up.

Pete came round after lunch, and it was nice to have him all to myself again. We went for a walk, and had a cappuccino down the street, and then he and Dad sat down together to do some work while I read for the millionth time about black troopers in Queensland in the nineteenth century.

I put my books away early, though — I'd decided to help Mum with dinner. Have you ever noticed that about studying? All the things you really hate doing suddenly become that things you really want to do, right now — just so you won't have to study any more. I was getting so much better at cooking since I'd started Year 12. I'd even actually done the ironing a couple of times.

So we had our dinner, and Dad and Pete told me how good it was. I didn't tell them that in the end all I'd done was cut up the veges and stir the sauce, and Mum just went, 'Mmm. You've done a great job, Kate.'

'Thanks,' I said. What else could I say?

Afterwards Pete and I went down to my room. Every now and then Dad would go past and bang really loudly on the door and then open it. I wasn't supposed to have Pete in my room with the door shut, just in cause we — you know — *did* something. I shut it all the time, of course. And

Dad opened it all the time. Still, we managed to enjoy ourselves in between — sometimes kissing, sometimes talking, sometimes just sitting in my armchair with our arms round each other. And later on, as usual, I walked him out to the gate.

While we were standing there, basically not wanting the night to finish, I remembered something I'd read the other day, in a book about Shakespeare's life, about him having had a lady mistress and a male lover. I thought it was pretty interesting — and about ten thousand times more interesting than alpha meets hyperbolic axis. But as soon as I'd got halfway through my first sentence, Pete cut in.

'Don't start with all that, Katie. I have enough of it when I'm studying. If I hear another word about that bastard Shakespeare I'm going to puke.'

Which pretty much put a damper on my story.

Of course, when it was time to go he gave me a big hug. 'I love you,' he said.

'I love you,' I said. And I did.

But I couldn't help being a bit disappointed.

Chapter 14

A t school on Monday Jamie told me he'd talked to Suzy, and it was fine if Pete wanted to come along. I can't say the news thrilled me. This was a whole new set of problems for me. I really wanted to go to that dinner. I just wanted the chance to be with people like me. But I knew I couldn't take Pete along. Well, I could, of course, but he'd have a terrible time — and I'd have a terrible time because he was having a terrible time. But I also knew that if I told him I was going and didn't want him to come — well, you can imagine how he'd feel.

'I thought that'd be good news,' Jamie said.

'Mmm,' I said.

'You don't have to come, Kate. I just thought it might be something you'd like.'

'It is! That is, I think it would be.'

'Then what's the problem?'

Could I tell him? I really didn't like the thought that there were any problems between Pete and me. It even made me feel a bit sick. It'd all been so simple and beautiful — I couldn't imagine anything going wrong. Ever. Not that this was the end of the world, I guess. Even if I'd told Pete about the party, and he'd said he didn't want to go and asked me not to — well, I would've stayed with him, and everything would've been all right. I would have been a bit disappointed, but everything would've been okay.

But the thing now, the thing that was making me feel a bit queasy, was that I wanted to go — and I wanted to go without Pete. But how could I tell Jamie that? How could I even say it out loud? I didn't even want to think it. But it was true.

Jamie was still looking at me like he expected an answer, so I just said, 'Can I think about it for a while?'

'Sure.' He looked at me for a minute like he wanted to say something else, but all he said was, 'Just let me know by Thursday, so I can let Suzy know how many she has to feed.'

I nodded. I felt too miserable to speak.

What was I going to do? It wasn't as if I didn't still love Pete. My heart hurt every time I thought about him, and the thought of being without him made me really panic. I didn't know what I'd do without him. I lay awake for hours on Monday night, thinking about it all. It wasn't even just whether I'd go to the party or not — and if I did, how I'd do it — though that was a problem enough. What really kept me awake was just the thought of Pete and me — how much I loved him, and at the same time what a nuisance loving him was. And then I'd lie awake a bit more, just feeling guilty about all the things I'd been thinking about before.

He came round on Tuesday night, and I felt like a real traitor. I wanted to burst into tears and go down on my knees and beg him to forgive me — even though I hadn't actually done anything. It seemed to me that just thinking about doing something he wouldn't like was a pretty serious crime. But I didn't do anything of those things. Instead I was just as nice to him as I could be, and we ended up having a really good night. And that's when I decided I wouldn't go to Suzy's.

Jamie was away on Wednesday, so I couldn't tell him I wouldn't be there on Saturday. But I went through the whole day feeling pretty pleased with myself. What was a party compared to the love of my life? Loving was about giving, my dad always said.

But then a strange thing started to happen. I think it had something to do with 'LA Law', believe it or not. I was sitting there watching it after dinner, with *Europe Since 1870* open on my lap (just in case the desire to know more about Imperial Britain's expansionist policy suddenly overcame me), watching these glamorous career women making difficult decisions, and their husbands and boyfriends being all understanding and supportive — and I started to feel cheated.

I mean, why should I have to give up what I wanted, just because Pete thought Shakespeare was a suck? Just because I loved Pete, didn't mean my whole life had to revolve around him, did it? Hadn't I spent two of the worst days of my life at the football, just to please him? Not to mention a total of probably about a thousand hours now, sitting on the front fence in sub-zero temperatures, listening to him go on and on about the molecular structure of chicken satay or something. I deserved to go to that party. Didn't I?

So *that* night I decided I would go, and Pete could like it — or — well, hopefully he wouldn't mind too much. And I went to sleep feeling pretty good about myself.

Thursday Jamie was back at school, and I told him I would be going on Saturday — by myself.

He looked surprised.

'Pete not interested?'

'Mmm,' I said.

I still hadn't decided exactly what I was going to do about Pete. But I'd be seeing him tonight — I was bound to think of the best way to explain things by then. I hoped.

But Pete arrived that afternoon, and dinner came and went, and he sat down to do some work with Dad — and I still hadn't been able to decide what I was going to say to him. While he was working, I went down to my room and practiced a few lines. Like:

'Pete, I've been invited to this dinner at Suzy Campbell's place. I'd really like to go, but there'll be mostly uni students there...'

'There's this dinner at Suzy Campbell's place on Saturday — she asked me if I wanted to go, and I do — but...'

'I won't be able to see you on Saturday, Pete. Suzy Campbell's invited me to her place and...'

The problem with these great lines was that I couldn't work out a way of finishing them. What could I say? And I don't want you to come? And you'd have a really bad time because you wouldn't understand what we were talking about? I just couldn't think of a polite way of saying what I wanted to say. It was awful, because for the first time ever I felt like there was something I couldn't talk to Pete about.

So in the end I just let him go without saying anything.

I really wanted to ask someone's advice, but who? I almost told Mum, but I knew what she'd say — Be Honest. Great. I wanted to be honest, but how could I? I thought about asking Jamie but I knew he'd just say don't worry about it. Which wasn't much help either.

So, you know what I did in the end? Even now I can't believe it. It was a terrible thing to do — and cowardly too — but at the time I had the best intentions in the world. I just didn't want to hurt Pete's feelings, and I couldn't think of any way of telling him the truth without doing that. So when he rang on Saturday morning to ask what I wanted to do that night — well — I pretended I was sick. I told him I wasn't going to do anything, just lie in bed all day. And with any luck I'd be better again on Sunday, so I could see him then.

He offered to come round and sit with me, but I told him I'd probably just sleep. And then I got off the phone really quickly. I couldn't bear it any more. I did go back to bed after that, I felt so terrible. I slept for a little while, then I lay there a bit longer, trying to convince myself I'd done the right thing. And I did, too, in the end. I just kept telling myself all this bullshit like, it's better that he doesn't know about it, and there's no harm done. Stuff like that. And eventually — mainly because I wanted to — I convinced myself.

I'd like to be able to say I ended up having a terrible time, feeling guilty about lying to Pete and sneaking round behind his back. But I didn't. I had a ball.

Around seven I slipped into my best little black number, and a bit after that Jamie came and picked me up. We were about the fourth or fifth people there, which was just right. Not so early that you feel like a complete dag, but early enough so that you get to meet people as they arrive, instead of walking into a room full of strangers. Most of the people there except Jamie were a year or so older than me, but that wasn't a problem. They were all really friendly.

There weren't any of those life-long friendships that were always a problem at school. There, no matter how well you got to know someone — and there were a few people there I knew pretty well now — you could never quite join that inner circle. You just hadn't been around long enough.

But these people had all met at the beginning of the year. They didn't know anything about each other's families, and not much about each

135

other's lives. They came from all over the place, too — there were even a couple of people from the country, like me. Though not from anywhere so far from anywhere else. But I even had a chance to talk about where I was from, and how I'd grown up. For the first time I felt like it wasn't something to be ashamed of. Everyone seemed to think it was pretty interesting, really.

And we talked about books and history and poetry, and all sorts of things I'd never dare open my mouth about normally, with the people I usually hung around with. I can't tell you how good it felt to be able to do that, and not feel like a complete jerk.

And it was good to spend some time with Jamie again, away from school. At school these days almost all we talked about was work — whether we'd finished our assignment, how study was going, or what a jerk Mr Hall was. It was good to get away from all that, and not think once about passing or failing. And I did end up acting as his interpreter.

So all in all I had a great night. While I was there I forgot about everything else, about school and home and Pete. I felt like I was just me — not a student or a girlfriend or a daughter. Just a person. I liked it. It felt good.

Chapter 15

I have to admit I didn't feel quite so great when I woke up on Sunday morning. The good feelings were starting to wear off, and the guilt was starting to come back. So I lay in bed for a while, convincing myself that it didn't really matter, and I'd call Pete straight after breakfast, and then I got up.

But as soon as I got to the kitchen I knew something was wrong. I said good morning, and Mum and Dad said good morning, but they were looking pretty serious about their muesli, and after they'd looked at me they kind of looked at each other and went quiet. I poured myself some coffee from the pot, and sat down at the table. I wanted to ask what was wrong but I was afraid to. After a little while, and some more looks at

Dad, Mum said, 'Pete dropped round last night. To see how you were feeling.'

I held onto my coffee cup really tightly, and I could feel my face getting really, really warm. I couldn't bear to look at them. I didn't know what to say. We were all quiet for a while, then Dad said — not angry, you know, more sort of sad, 'That wasn't a very nice thing to do, Katie.'

'I know.' My voice was really small and squeaky. I felt like I was going to cry. There was more silence, then it was Mum's turn again.

'Katie, we've always tried to teach you how important honesty is...' She looked down at her plate. 'There's a reason for that, you know. It's not some old-fashioned idea your grandparents found in the Bible. It's to stop people being hurt. No matter how ugly the truth is, it's never as bad as feeling you've been deceived. Especially by the people we love.'

I'd let go of my coffee cup and was hugging myself really tightly now, and tears were running down my face. My head was a great mess of thoughts — about how much I loved Pete, and how much he'd loved (and trusted) me, how he must've felt last night while I was out enjoying myself. How he must hate me now.

I couldn't bear it any more. I jumped up from the table, ran down to my room, sat down against the door I'd just slammed, and howled. I cried and cried until my head and chest ached and my eyes were burning. After a while I crawled over to the bed and climbed in and cried some more, with the blankets over my head, hugging my knees against my chest. My heart really ached — and not just for Pete, who I must've really hurt — but for me too, because it looked like I'd just ruined one of the best things that'd ever happened in my life.

Eventually I stopped. I was just too tired. I lay there under the blankets for a while, and I slept a little bit. When I woke up I didn't exactly feel better, but I felt a bit more in control of myself. Mum and Dad just left me alone. I had a shower and got dressed, then walked over to Pete's place. I had to see him. I couldn't talk to him on the phone now.

When I arrived, his mum told me to go straight down to his rom. He was sitting at his desk, staring out the window. He didn't even look around. So I just stood in the doorway, looking at the back of his head and shoulders, remembering what it felt like to touch his hair and the back of his neck, and to put my arms round his shoulders. My eyes started to sting again, but I didn't cry. I just said, 'Hi.'

He turned round and looked at me. 'What do

you want?'

'I wanted to say I'm sorry.'

He looked back out the window.

'I *am* sorry.'

'For what?' he said to the window.

'For not being honest with you.'

'Really? Or are you just sorry I found out about it?'

I could see it wasn't going to be easy. Still, if I was going to do this, I might as well do it properly.

'Both,' I said.

'So it would've been all right if I'd stayed away like I was supposed to, and you'd gone off and done — whatever it was you did — if I'd never known!'

'No! I was sorry the moment I woke up this morning — sorry the minute I did it!'

'Not sorry enough to call me back and tell me the truth!'

'I couldn't!'

He sat there, very stiff, sort of rigid in his chair, then finally said, 'What couldn't you tell me? Some other bloke asked you out, I suppose.'

'Of course not! What do you think I am?'

'I don't know anything about you. Before yesterday I thought... I would've said...'

But he didn't say what he would've said. He

just stood up, and started fiddling with the things on his desk. I went over and tried to look him in the face, but all I could get was his profile. I'd never seen him look like that before. It was scary. I tried to put my arm round him, but he slapped my hand away.

'Don't touch me, you — slut!'

Although it wasn't easy, I'd been trying to stay calm, but that really made me lose my temper.

'Don't you dare call me a slut!'

'What else am I supposed to think, when you go sneaking off behind my back? What else could there be that you couldn't tell me about?'

'There's a million things I couldn't tell you about — because you're just not interested! You don't care about anything except your stupid football and your stupid mates and your stupid bloody chemical equations! If you'd stopped for one minute and listened to some of the things I tried to tell you about, none of this would've happened!'

'What are you talking about?'

'If you really wanted to know what I was doing last night, I was at Suzy Campbell's having dinner with some friends of hers, and talking about books. And if I'd thought for one second you'd be interested — or even pretend to be interested, for my sake — I would've asked you to come too!'

'Great! So now you're embarrassed to introduce me to your friends! I'm not good enough
for you!'

He was looking me straight in the face now,
and I wished he wouldn't.

'Kate, you're not just a liar — you're a selfish,
stuck-up bitch!'

I couldn't bear it any more. I didn't say
anything, I just ran out of the room and out of the
house, and ran pretty much all the way home.

But by the time I'd reached the park in Bridge
Street, I was out of breath so I had to walk the
last couple of blocks. I couldn't believe what'd
just happened. I'd never seen Pete mad before —
never seen him lose his temper at all, not with
anyone. And even when I only first knew him,
I'd never imagined him being angry with me.
Embarrassed by me, or ashamed of me, or just not
wanting to have much to do with me — but not
absolutely furious. It was a terrible feeling, and
scary, too.

It hadn't seemed such a big deal at the time.
I knew it was the wrong thing to do, but it
hadn't seemed like a big thing. I'd just been
trying to avoid exactly the kind of thing that'd
just happened — without missing out on what I
wanted to do. It didn't seem so criminal. I knew

that if I'd asked Pete to go with me, he would've said no — and wouldn't have wanted me to go either. And if I'd told him I wanted to go alone, he would've acted pretty much like he did this afternoon. Maybe not quite so angry, but still pretty pissed off.

Was I a snob? I didn't feel like one. I'd never thought I was one. To me, snobs were people who thought they were better than everyone else — and that certainly wasn't me. Just the opposite, most of the time. I didn't feel like I was any better than Pete, that's for sure. But if I *had* asked Pete to go with me, and he'd said yes — what would I have felt like then? Was I really just trying to save him from a boring night? Or was he right — would I have been embarrassed to be with him at a place like that?

I really didn't know the answer to that one. I felt like I didn't know anything any more. Mainly I just felt kind of numb.

When I got home, Mum and Dad were hanging around, looking pretty anxious. What could I say to them? 'I've completely stuffed things up, I'm a horrible person, and Pete's never going to speak to me again'? I was a bit worried that one of them would start going on about the value of honesty again. But they didn't say a word.

That was worse than anything. I almost wished they'd nag at me, or say something really unfair, just so I could feel like I wasn't the only one doing the wrong thing. But all they did was look at me, sort of sad. I couldn't bear it.

I went to my room without saying anything — it was pretty bad in there too. The bed was all messed up and there were tissues everywhere from where I'd been crying, and my dress from last night was on the floor. It was too much. I scrunched the dress up and stuffed it in the rubbish bin. I never wanted to look at it again. Then I picked up all the grotty tissues and shoved them in on top of it, and straightened the bed. I would've liked to have another cry, but I couldn't be bothered. What was the point? It was all over. It was all my fault, and it was all over, and crying wasn't going to make one bit of difference.

So instead I sat down at my desk and took out *Pride and Prejudice* and sat there staring at it. After a while I thought I might try writing a letter to Pete — you know, try to explain things without yelling, and without him yelling at me.

I guess I must've had about ten goes at that. And each time I got about two pages into it, and then threw it away. It was too complicated. I didn't know myself if he was right or wrong, or what was going on. I couldn't even properly explain why I did what I did — it'd just seemed like the only thing to do at the time.

So in the end I gave up, and just sat there staring out the window into the street. Aftar a while it got dark, and a while after that Mum came in to tell me dinner was ready.

'I'm not hungry.'

'You should try and eat something, sweet-heart.'

'I'll be sick if I try and eat anything.'

She looked like she wanted to say something, but I just stared at her, and after a while she just patted my hand and went away.

It must've been about ten o'clock when I realised I was freezing cold. And when I realised I was cold it made me think about sitting on the front fence and shivering, listening to Pete talk about science. When I thought about that, I almost felt like I was going to cry again. I got kind of choked up, but nothing much else happened. Maybe your body needs some time to make tears. Maybe I needed to drink a few glasses of water or something. I don't know. I didn't care very much. I felt like I'd never really care about anything again.

I didn't bother putting the light on. I just got undressed and got into bed.

After a while Dad came in. He didn't say

anything. He just sat on the edge of the bed. He smoothed my hair a bit, and then he held my hand.

And that's how I went to sleep.

Chapter 16

It was weird going to school on Monday. It was weird seeing all the same people I knew, the same as ever. The same old routine, the same old classes — and feeling like my life had changed for ever. Which is a bit of a cliche, but that's really how I felt.

Jamies was full of beans and all ready to talk about Saturday night. I told him to shut up, and then was sorry I'd been so rude. But Jamie's good that way. You know how I said nothing seems to worry him much? Well, he didn't take that personally either — he just knew straight away something was wrong. He put his arm around me and we walked down to the end of the oval, pretty much out of sight. And then I burst into tears again.

Now, a lot of guys freak out when a girl starts crying. But Jamie just put both his arms round me, and I leant on his shoulder, and left mascara marks all over his shirt. But he didn't mind that. And when he said, 'What's the matter?' and I said 'I don't want to talk about it' — he didn't mind that either. And he helped me clean up my face before the next class. He didn't ask any questions. He just said, 'I thought you'd got to be all sophisticated and metropolitan — but deep down you're still a dag, aren't you?'

Which made me smile.

I'd only been home about half an hour when there was a knock on the door. It was Pete. I felt strange when I saw him. He looked — the same. That was the weird thing. He looked like just the same old Pete. Only everything was different.

'Can I talk to you?' he said.

'Sure.'

I let him in, and we went down to my room and shut the door. No one came and bashed on it this time.

'I wanted to say — sorry — for the things I said yesterday.'

'No — it was my fault. I should never have done it.'

'But you were right — if I'd been more interested in the things you're interested in, it would never have happened.'

'I still shouldn't have lied to you… but thanks.'

I held his hand, and we just sat there for a minute.

'The thing is… I'm *not* interested in — books and things. And you're not really interested in the things I like any more, are you?'

'Not really.'

He squeezed my hand tighter than ever. 'Pretty soon we won't have anything at all to talk about, you know.'

'I know.'

'I don't… I'm not angry with you… but I've been thinking.'

'Me too.'

He put his arm round me. 'Do you think maybe it's time we… gave it a rest?'

'You're right,' I said. And he was. But it still made me feel kind of sick to say it.

We just sat on the edge of the bed for a while with our arms round each other. Finally he said, 'Well, I guess I'd better be going.'

'Okay.'

I walked with him to the front door, and then out to the gate, for old time's sake. We both stood there for minute, looking at each other, then at the ground, then at each other. Then he held out his arms, and I put mine around him, and we hugged each other really tightly.

'Bye bye, Katie,' he whispered. His voice sounded funny. 'Thanks for everything.'

'Bye,' I squeaked. I was trying hard not to cry. 'Thank *you*.'

But in the end we both cried a bit. I wanted to tell him how much I loved him. But I didn't. Instead we both just cried a bit, and kissed a bit, and then said goodbye. And I watched him walk up the street from my house for the last time.

When I went back inside Mum was in the kitchen, putting the kettle on.

'Have you two patched things up?' she asked.

'Nope,' I said.

She came round and gave me a hug. 'Katie, I'm sorry.'

'Me too.'

She sat me down in a chair. 'Let's have a cup of tea.'

We didn't drink tea much at home, except when my grandmother came to visit. But it was kind of soothing, and it seemed the right thing to do, something different, when everything else in my life had changed. Everything important, anyway.

'Do you want to talk about it?' Mum asked. I shook my head.

So we just sat there for a minute, drinking our

tea, and then in a while Mum started talking about her vege patch, and some of the kids she teaches. By the time I got up from the table I felt much better.

It'd be too much to say that from then on everything was all right. There were still times — lot of times — when I felt so terrible I wanted to lay down and die. And the first few days at school, when everyone was finding out that Pete and I had broken up, were really awful. You know, people kept coming up to me looking really serious and saying things like, 'I'm sooooo sorry' or 'Are you okay?' It wasn't easy.

But over the next few weeks there were less and less terrible times, and if I didn't feel exactly happy, at least I wasn't one hundred per cent miserable. What made it easier was thinking about all the good that'd come out of knowing Pete. I felt good about myself. I felt like I'd learned a lot — just about how to get on in the world — and I felt like I'd helped Pete out too. Even if it did backfire a bit in the end.

And then there were just all the great times we'd had together. It wasn't a good idea to think about that stuff too much at the moment, but I knew that sooner or later I'd be able to enjoy all those memories, without getting too choked up.

Studying helped too. I was just too busy to

Titles to enjoy in the *Lovelines* series

think about much else. Before I knew it exams had arrived. English was our first one. Which wasn't too bad for me — it was nice to start with something I felt pretty confident about.

On the big day I was sitting in the kitchen trying to swallow my toast, when the phone rang.

'Hello?'

'Katie? It's Pete.'

My heart did a little flip.

'How are you feeling?'

'Okay,' I said. 'How about you?'

'Not too bad. Thanks to you.'

'Don't thank me — you did all the work. I told you you could.'

'Yeah, well — I wouldn't be here if it wasn't for you. I just wanted to say thanks again. And good luck.'

'Thanks, Pete. And good luck to you too.'

We hung up.

Mum walked past a minute later. She stopped and gave me a look.

'Katie? Do you feel all right?'

'Yeah,' I said. 'Yeah. I feel good.'